## "I heard something."

Kara drew Millie to her as Phil began to growl. "Phil did, too."

Beau whispered in her ear, "It came from behind that crooked tree. I'm going to check." Every nerve in his body was electric.

Kara nodded her understanding, gave Phil the silent command and tapped a finger to Millie's head to convey the same message. Phil stopped growling, but the scruff on his neck rose. He wouldn't let anyone close to her or Millie. Comforting, unless the intruder had a weapon.

Beau turned and crept into the darkest of the shadows, easing his way to the stump one careful step following another. The damp soil muffled the sound of his boots as he drew closer. The slow creep was excruciating and necessary, like controlling the dust signature of a massive vehicle packed with soldiers. Stay invisible as long as possible. He eased his gun out. There was someone there in the shifting shadows. He could feel it, a presence, human and malignant.

This stalker was going to come clean. Right here and right now.

**Dana Mentink** is a nationally bestselling author. She has been honored to win two Carol Awards, a HOLT Medallion and an RT Reviewers' Choice Best Book Award. She's authored more than thirty novels to date for Love Inspired Suspense and Harlequin Heartwarming. Dana loves feedback from her readers. Contact her at danamentink.com.

# FOLLOWING THE CLUES

## DANA MENTINK

**LOVE INSPIRED SUSPENSE**
INSPIRATIONAL ROMANCE

**LOVE INSPIRED® SUSPENSE**
INSPIRATIONAL ROMANCE

ISBN-13: 978-1-335-63875-5

Following the Clues

Copyright © 2025 by Dana Mentink

Recycling programs for this product may not exist in your area.

For questions and comments about the quality of this book, please contact us at CustomerService@Harlequin.com.

Love Inspired
22 Adelaide St. West, 41st Floor
Toronto, Ontario M5H 4E3, Canada
www.LoveInspired.com

**Printed in Lithuania**

MIX
Paper | Supporting responsible forestry
FSC® C021394

While we look not at the things which are seen,
but at the things which are not seen:
for the things which are seen are temporal;
but the things which are not seen are eternal.
—*2 Corinthians* 4:18

To the hardworking staff and volunteers
at Joybound People & Pets. Thank you for giving
the animals and their owners a second chance at love,
and to vet tech Emily for her care and mighty courage.

# ONE

Kara Wolfe's joy turned to fear.

One moment she was massaging her blood-hound Millie's saggy head, settling her in the back seat with her companion and guide, Phil, an enormous white Anatolian shepherd. The next, she and the dog were diving into the tangled bushes, out of the way of a rusty van that suddenly erupted onto the trail. The van barely cleared her vehicle as it clattered by, spewing mud.

Kara landed painfully on her stomach, Millie beside her.

Before she'd even managed to roll over, Phil dove out of the open car window, barking furiously at the vanishing van. He chased it for a few yards, until he barreled back to his charges. Kara sat up, waving Phil off. "I'm all right, boy."

He anxiously examined Millie, sniffing and licking his charge until he was satisfied she was uninjured also. Millie gazed in his direction with her filmy eyes and indulged his fussing. Millie was almost completely blind, so the accident had probably frightened her badly.

Kara groaned as she observed the ripped knee of her jeans. What had just happened? They were on a lonely trail outside of Whisper Valley, her hometown in the wilds of Northern California, certainly not a convenient shortcut for any driver. The out-of-the-way location was why she chose the spot to do some scent work with Millie and Phil, Millie's guide.

She got up, brushed the leaves from her clothes and picked a branch from her long hair. And why, she huffed as she took inventory, hadn't the guy stopped to see if he'd caused injury or worse?

It wasn't likely the driver of the van had intentionally tried to run them down. Wno would even know a woman and her two dogs were conducting a training run on a muddy seldom-used road? Didn't excuse them from not stopping though. She took a couple of pictures of the ruts the van's tires had left in the earth, but it was a cursory effort. She'd call the police from the car when she could get a signal, but they wouldn't be able to do much. Her primary goal was to hurry to her next stop, then get back to Security Hounds Ranch safely with her two canine partners. She loaded the dogs quickly.

Her breathing was still hitched from the near

catastrophe as she carefully piloted her SUV toward the main route, relieved when the trail ended. She hit the brakes before entering the one-lane frontage road, instantly catching sight of a sea blue truck approaching, the wipers slapping away at the spritzing rain.

Big Blue.

She gaped in disbelief, instantly plunged into a memory.

Beau O'Connor's deep voice, unusually soft for such a big man. "Big Blue's the best set of wheels in Siskiyou County." His image was blurred in her mind, receding into the past in the seven months since she'd seen him on his last disastrous leave from the Marines. After their relaxed dinner together where he'd teased her about being a vegetarian, and she'd returned in kind about the massive steak he'd devoured, he'd gone home to his mother's place, and everything had exploded. Her information was sketchy since Beau hadn't spoken to her after, but she'd heard the replay of the 911 call.

*Reporting an attack.*

Beau's concise speech spoke of his military training, as did his description of the area, a spot overlooking his mother's fish hatchery property. But the details of what he'd witnessed were unclear, a figure in dark clothes, strangling another, both appeared to be males, one wearing a yellow sweatshirt. The police had told him to wait until they arrived, but of course he hadn't. No, Beau was the person she'd known since the fourth grade who'd once chased a pedestrian for ten blocks in the sizzling heat to return a wallet he'd left at the bus stop. Beau didn't wait when he could act.

Beau had sustained a head injury. He'd been transported to the hospital. She'd not been allowed to see him for the first few days, and then when the police and doctors were done, Beau had mystifyingly declined any and all visitors. A week later he'd checked himself out of the hospital and left without a single word of explanation. She'd not heard a thing from him since, in spite of her calls and texts.

She blinked as the familiar blue truck passed her. Was it actually Beau behind the sunglasses underneath the brim of the baseball cap? He'd returned home, again without so much as a message to her. Her heart squeezed, and for the millionth time she wondered what she'd done that caused him to sever their friendship.

Sure, there had been distance between them since she'd started dating Kyle, his best friend, her junior year of high school. That space only widened with their engagement several years later and more so when Kyle was diagnosed with leukemia and subsequently passed away.

But four years had gone by since the funeral, and she and Beau had restarted their friendship, texting, emailing. And always when he'd returned on leave, they'd have a meal and laugh about the past, even if they did avoid any talk about Kyle. They were friends, always would be, or so she'd believed.

*Wrong, Kara. Obviously.*

Though her eyes grew misty, she determinedly gripped the wheel. Beau didn't have a problem ejecting her from his circle after he'd been injured. It made keeping the secret his mother had entrusted her with easier for Kara's conscience.

An engine rumbled and Phil and Millie straightened. In the distance, another vehicle flew around the turn. She gaped. The rusty van again.

Its windows were smeared with mud, as well as the front license plate.

The wheels skidded as the van tore up the road. What was the driver doing? Had they been up the mountain trail, lying in wait until Beau came along? The little hairs on the back of her neck prickled as it flew past her, sped up, encroaching on the truck. Quickly she pulled out behind the reckless van, honking the horn, desperate to warn Beau he was about to be hit.

"Look out!" she yelled uselessly. The truck continued on at a regular pace, maddeningly unaware of the danger approaching. She lay on the horn, sending the two dogs into a frenzy.

Powerless, she watched as the van smashed full speed into the truck's rear, sending it lurching forward before it eased off a pace. She sped up. Incredibly, the van shimmied into position for another attack.

She screamed. Both dogs barked at full volume.

Another smash from the van crumpled the truck's rear, shattering the taillight, sending pieces of red plastic dancing through the air. The truck skidded sideways off the asphalt toward the shoulder. She craned her neck to see around the van.

The tree... Big Blue was going to hit the tree.

At the absolute last second, the truck driver managed to wrestle the vehicle to the side so the impact was more glancing than head on. A scrape of metal sounded through her open window and the skid of brakes as Big Blue came to a halt.

The van sped past, rear plates obscured to the point that she could not get one measly digit. She pulled in a shaky breath and guided her car to a stop on the shoulder.

"Stay, dogs." She heard Millie bark as she unbuckled. Phil shoved his head through the open glass to watch her. He would leap out in a flash if she needed him.

She jogged over and skidded to a stop, heart pounding as the truck door was flung open, and a man climbed out, tall, handsome in jeans, flannel shirt and boots. Beau O'Connor.

It really was him, his six-six frame thinner than she remembered, a carpet of stubble hiding his chin. Strange. Since he'd turned eighteen she'd never seen him anything but clean-shaven, hair cut military short. There was no concealing the iridescent blue of his irises, the brows a shade lighter than the hair that now touched his ears, wavy around the temples. He fisted his hands on his hips and surveyed the scraped paint and mashed bumper.

"Are...are you okay?" she managed.

He jerked a cursory look at her as if he hadn't realized she was there.

"Yes." He scrubbed a hand over his chin, scanned her vehicle and the surrounding area. "You all right? You didn't get hit?"

"No." She could hardly get the word out. There was such a distance between them, as if he were a stranger rather than someone she'd known since childhood. "You should call the police."

"I will." He ran a palm over the dented side, jaw tight. "That's gonna cost me a bundle to repair and repaint. At least she's drivable." He surveyed the road again. "Thanks for stopping, by the way. That was decent of you."

*Decent?*

The barking dogs caught his attention. "Your hounds are on duty. That's good." He yanked his driver's door open. "I'd better be going, if you're sure you're not hurt, that is."

"No. Not hurt." He watched as she made her way back to her car. "I… I didn't know you'd come back to town."

He paused, taking a half step back, wary. "Uh, yeah. Just arrived yesterday morning."

Questions choked her.

*What happened after you went to the hospital?*

*And why are you pretending you don't even know me?*

A lump formed in her throat.

He looked pained. "Sorry to hustle. Gotta track down my mom. Nice talking to you."

"But…" She gaped. "You can't just leave. Someone almost killed you a few moments ago. I think they planned it. I saw them up the trail. You need to file a police report."

"I will. I promise. Thanks a lot, you know, for stopping." Again, he smiled in that weary way. "Most people wouldn't."

Kara almost argued. Most everyone, in her mind, would stop and render help in such a situation. And definitely for a longtime friend. She was still grappling with what to say.

He got into the truck and shot another look

at her, those clear blue eyes simultaneously familiar and strange, shadowed now, as if storm clouds had come to rest behind the irises. With an elbow propped on the window, he paused as though he wanted to say something, his brows gathering into a puzzled V.

She got into her car. Then he waved and guided the truck back onto the road and drove away.

She stared after him, the man who'd been a best friend to her and her fiancé. And he'd just treated her as if they were newly acquainted. Both dogs were agitated now, wanting her to take them home.

But she continued to gaze in the direction in which Big Blue had disappeared.

Someone was after him, no matter what he believed.

But that only accounted for a portion of her shock.

Unless Beau was a brilliant actor, his blank look had been sincere.

Beau O'Connor didn't know who she was.

Beau detected a rattle in his truck's chassis when he eased along the river, which was full and swift as it flowed down from the foothills of Mount Shasta. He was angry about the hit-and-run, but nothing poked a hole in his growing agitation. He probably should have called the cops about the accident right then, but he didn't have the bandwidth. His worry was a low-grade throb, but it was creeping higher with every passing hour. Where was his mother? He hadn't gleaned any helpful information in town from the workers at the gas station or the coffee shop, and the grocery hadn't clapped eyes on her for a few days.

His thoughts ran like the river as he drove the mountain pass to his family property, rambling back in time, to a girl he'd known and maybe even loved. Her nickname was Henny Penny. He remembered the school prom, how he'd fretted about the cost of tickets and tuxes and corsages, silently dithering until Kyle, his best friend, had asked the hazel-eyed Henny Penny. He'd stayed home.

Beau had joined the Marines. Kyle had almost become a dentist, but he'd gotten sick. No one's life had gone to plan, especially Beau's when, seven months prior, he'd been injured right here on the hatchery grounds. He thought of Henny Penny's phone calls, which he'd left unanswered, the messages that he'd listened to from his hospital bed. The texts he'd deleted without replying.

What he'd witnessed back in November had cost him dearly.

*What you thought you witnessed*, he corrected.

The tape played in his mind again, the choking sound of an airway being throttled, a groan, his own shout at the figures grappling in the deep shadows of the cedar trees, his feet running through the grass past the equipment shed, a blinding pain to his head.

He'd awakened in the hospital, the local sheriff patiently explaining there had been no evidence found of a crime on his mother's property. He'd likely fallen, struck his head. He'd learned shortly thereafter that his brain had been injured to the point where he would not be able to return to the Marines. A snap of the fingers and his life was reduced to wreckage.

It wasn't that his circumstances were better now, seven months later. His body had recovered even if his brain hadn't, but he'd finally listened to his mother. "Look, Beau," she'd said, "sooner or later you've got to put whatever happened behind you. Marines don't run, do they?"

That last bit stung. He'd been hunkering down in a buddy's empty trailer, not running exactly, but hiding, which amounted to the same thing. Her words woke him up and he suddenly knew what he had to do. Start over. Learn how to live again in a place that was the only home he knew. A new mission.

He recalled his boot camp instructor's motto. *Sweat dries, blood clots, bones heal.*

But what if his brain didn't?

And that terrifying thought reminded him of

the other thing his instructor said. *The spineless need not apply.* So he was home. And he would start over, and the first mission was to help his mother with Pioneer Day, a community event only four days away.

He'd arrived Tuesday, the day before, and found no sign of her, no note to indicate her whereabouts. He'd dumped his gear in the tiny guest room in the residence above the hatchery office, started on fixing the fence he'd noticed was damaged as he'd driven in and tried to keep his mind far away from what had happened the last time he'd visited.

Wednesday morning his mother had still not made an appearance. Two of the employees, a married couple, were off on vacation for a few days, and the one still on, Vince Greyson, was away seeding a creek with their prize Eagle Lake trout, according to the delivery schedule on his mom's computer. Fortunately, she'd never changed the password. It was a nine-hour drive, so Vince would bunk at a hotel rather than immediately return to the hatchery. Their phone call that morning hadn't shed any light either.

"Beau?" Vince had said. He had a deep voice that Beau had often thought would be perfect on the radio. "Heard you were coming back, finally. Good, 'cuz there's been a ton that needs fixing around here. Has been for a while now."

Beau heard the underlying criticism. *Why didn't you come help out as soon as you were medically retired from the Marines months ago?*

A fair question.

"Where's Mom? She's not answering her cell."

"Dunno. She doesn't clear her schedule with me," Vince had said testily. "Could be she took on a delivery and didn't write it down. But while you're waiting for her, see what you can do about the pump in Pond B, huh? I got enough on my plate."

The pump had required sweaty effort with a wrench and a can of oil, but he'd restored it to a healthy purr. Still no sign of his mother.

Hours after he'd been driven off the road, still with no indication of his mother's whereabouts and her phone going straight to voicemail, he drove back to the Pine Bluff Police Station to express his worry.

Statement taken, the formidable dark-haired sheriff cocked his head at Beau.

"We've met, you know?" he said. "I took your statement when you thought someone had been murdered at the hatchery, remember?"

Beau's cheeks went hot as he flicked a glance at the name tag. Todd Franco. He'd shaved off his mustache.

"Have I aged so much in seven months that

you didn't recognize me?" Franco's tone was joking, but there was a real question underneath.

"I remember you. Of course." He fumbled through his concerns about his mother.

"All right," Franco said. "I'll get the word out. Anything else you'd like to talk about?" Franco's eyes were ink dark, assessing.

He explained what had happened with the reckless van.

"You're just now getting around to reporting it?" He shrugged. "Got another witness statement earlier, fortunately. You were on my list to call about it."

Had to be a report from the lady who'd stopped to help him, the puzzled look on her face.

No, not only puzzled, hurt almost. Worry tickled his stomach, that perpetual anxiety that he'd lived with since he'd woken up in that hospital bed.

But all that mattered now was finding his mother. Phone stowed in his pocket, he headed in the direction of the hatchery to search the property one more time.

As Kara drove her napping dogs back to her family's ranch in Whisper Valley, her body felt slowed by shock, numb with disbelief as she struggled to process it all. Beau hadn't seemed nearly as upset about the reckless van driver as he was worried about his mother, Ree. Now Kara was worried too.

When Kara's father died of cancer, Ree had been the elementary school librarian in nearby Whisper Valley and Beth Wolfe's friend. Ree would fetch Kara before sunup and take her to the hatchery until it was time to head to town for school. Kara had nothing but gratitude and love for Ree. That's why she'd agreed to dust off her real estate license to help Ree when she'd asked. She'd told herself that was her motivation anyway.

Kara parked the vehicle in the Security Hounds driveway, unfastened Millie from the back seat and kissed her on the snout. The bloodhound's wriggly jowls slapped across Kara's chin as the dog bussed her back in slobbery fashion. Millie was always ready for some love. Phil, on the other hand, edged himself away from her affection. Phil wasn't one for physical gestures, but she imagined she saw a gleam of satisfaction in his black eyes anyway once they'd finally made it back to the homestead. He'd slink off to supervise the chicken coop, which had been his primary job until Kara had tried him out as Millie's companion. They had another shepherd watching the fowl now, but Phil couldn't quite stomach letting go.

*I know, Phil. Letting go is hard.*

"Great team effort, you two, in spite of the rough ending to our morning." After the bizarre roadside encounter, they'd stopped at the neighbor's property to check in on the elderly Nana Ethel, who'd wandered away the week before. Millie and her trusty companion Phil had found the lady in under two hours where she'd collapsed in a remote wooded area of the property. The grateful family had showered Millie with treats and a new dog sweater. Phil refused all his gifts, waiting until they were safely back in the car before he gulped his dog biscuit. Kara was too polite to tell the family that as long as Phil drew breath, that dog would never allow himself to be packed into a sweater. She couldn't even get him into the official Security Hounds harness, and since she only outweighed the dog by twenty pounds, she wasn't going to press the point.

Before she reached the porch step, Beth opened the door to the sprawling ranch style home and waved. Kara was thrilled to see that her mother, a retired Air Force nurse, had almost returned to her regular vigor as her spine mended from surgical repair. She unfurled towels to dry the dogs before Kara released Millie to the covered side yard while Phil streaked away to the chicken coop.

Kara reported on the dogs' training success.

"I knew if anybody could turn a blind dog and

that bruiser of a shepherd into an efficient team it would be you."

"Yes, they did great on the scent work," Kara said, "but something weird happened afterward."

Her mom frowned. "I'm beginning to think weird is the norm for this family."

True enough. Her sister, Steph, and her fiancé, Vance, and their dogs had narrowly escaped being murdered during a tracking and trailing competition in November. Steph, a tough ex-cop, still jumped at sudden noises, which everyone pretended not to notice.

They entered the house and the warmth was delightful. Kara stripped off her boots and socks, padded barefoot to the living room where Steph, Vance and Chase were assembled. Chase poked at the fire and Vance sat on the floor, stroking the three dogs lolling on the hearth rug. Chloe was Steph's champion bloodhound, snuggled between Millie and Pudge, Vance's oddball dog that looked as though he was made of leftover parts from other animals. Vance had brought Phil into the pack also.

Beth handed her a mug of her favorite herbal tea and a peanut butter sandwich for which she had no appetite. She related the details of the training session. The humans listened eagerly, especially when she got to the incident with Beau and the hit-and-run. "I reported it all in a call after I left Nana Ethel's family. I couldn't get a signal before then. I'll go back if the police need any more information."

Steph's shrewd eyes narrowed at Kara. "Let's have the rest, Sis. It's not just the reckless driver that's upsetting you. Was it seeing Beau again?"

She took a breath. "Yes, in a way. Ree didn't say anything about his return when I met with her."

Beth frowned. "Does his arrival have something to do with the project you're doing for Ree?"

"No. At least I don't think so." She hadn't disclosed the particulars of the favor Ree had asked of her even to her family, as Ree had requested. Taking up her real estate skills again was like pulling on a beloved scarf with an old scent lingering in the fabric. It was a fragile endeavor that she wasn't ready to disclose.

"What then?" Steph pressed.

"Of course it was upsetting, because I know he was targeted by the van driver, but something's wrong on top of that. He acted really weird. It was like…" She stopped, collecting her flyaway impressions. "It was like he didn't know who I was."

Chase stabbed at a burning log. "Guy needs to learn some manners. Anybody who would blow you off has a problem that needs correcting."

Kara shrugged, keeping her voice calm. "I

never understood why he left town without a word after that nasty business. I tried to contact him every way I could think of. Nothing. He just…vanished. Ree wouldn't talk about it."

"I visited Ree on several occasions after Vance was hospitalized too, and she just said he was 'dealing with some things.' Sort of put the kibosh on our relationship, actually," Beth said. "I got the feeling I made her uncomfortable. I haven't seen her except for a few awkward conversations where I got the distinct impression she didn't want to talk."

"Well, that's their loss then." Chase snagged half of Kara's untouched sandwich. "We've got other business to work on. How's the cargo heist case going?"

Vance laughed. "Piece of cake. Chloe and Pudge trailed the hijacker's scent right back to the trucking office. Inside job. Now we put together the report and talk to the cops and litigators. It'll tie us up for a while." He sighed. "The fun part is over."

"That's where I come in," Steph said with an eye roll. "For the mundane stuff, dotting i's and crossing t's."

Vance grinned. "No one dots and crosses like you do, my little buttercup."

Their laughter was cut short by Beth's phone ringing. She checked the screen.

"It's a call from Sheriff Franco." She answered and informed him he was on speaker.

"Good," he said. "Need a favor. Does your group have time for a search in Pine Bluff?"

Kara's pulse skipped up a notch. Pine Bluff... the location of Beau's family hatchery.

"We have teams available." Beth clicked open her phone to take notes.

"I don't know the whole picture yet. Could be all for nothing, but my gut's heaving, and I don't think it's just the burger I had for lunch. I know it's too late to search tonight, but do you have time to do me a favor tomorrow, early? County will reimburse your expenses and meet your fee if I authorize a search."

Beth sought the eyes of her family and everyone nodded. "Where do you need us?"

"The O'Connor Hatchery."

That tingling in Kara's nerves turned into a flood.

"Who's the missing person?" Beth said calmly.

There was a pause.

"Could be it's Ree O'Connor."

# TWO

After he tired of waiting for dawn, Beau drove his dented truck slowly, examining the property yet again.

A turn onto the neat, paved road brought him alongside the rearing channels, the long chutes with gently rippling water where the juvenile trout had a chance to mature after hatching. The channels were secured behind a heavy chain-link fence. The hatchery education building would be crammed from late June through August with visitors eager to observe the eggs hatching, the agile fry and the nursery ponds that cradled the older fish until they were ready to enter the raceways. At this ridiculously early hour, all was quiet.

The O'Connor Fish Hatchery had been his father Cal's brainchild, and his mother Ree laughingly told him on many occasions she thought Beau's dad had been a little loose in the brain for purchasing it. But the business had thrived, grown into a worldwide supplier of fish eggs, as well as the source of pond and lake stock for a large part of the state. It was a destination too, as his mother proudly proclaimed. Maybe not a fancy destination, but it boasted a visitor's area, complete with picnic tables and an education room for tour groups and kids' school excursions.

He rolled through the gates, skirting the two employee residences. Beau was proud of the Eagle Lake trout they raised, a native species threatened by diminished creek flow. He'd grown up with those little fry, run alongside them up the brood-stock ponds and watched them turn into beautiful, iridescent adults. The five million Eagle Lake trout eggs, along with the brown and rainbow trout they also raised, stocked countless state waterways.

Through his rolled down window, the scent of hay drifted in the predawn air. Over the hill, cozy in a stable on their neighbor's property, lived a dozen massively spoiled horses and mules.

As a young teen, he'd done every type of trout planting deliveries, including truck, air and even mule supply runs to remote mountain lakes. One sunny August day stood out in his memory, when the heat ate up the mountain coolness. The mule he was riding had been indifferent to both the warmth and the hefty container of finger-sized trout he was transporting to a lake tucked away at the bottom of a twisty valley. And his human traveling companion? A young lady who'd laughed and brushed the leaves from her hair and enjoyed the bumpy, sticky journey, the one he'd nicknamed Henny Penny for her love of birds of all kinds.

*Don't you have enough to think about right now?* Body sagging with fatigue and still no closer to finding his mother, he returned to the hatchery and brewed another pot of coffee, slugging it as he prowled through the office space, noting the to-do list written on the whiteboard. He tried not to think of how much work was waiting for him. Pioneer Day was coming on Sunday. It was a festival where their tiny town threw the doors especially wide to visitors. The hatchery would be a key part of the events, its picnic area and raised stage used for musical performances and the hatchery hosting "pick your fish" races. Silly, undoubtedly, but he'd eaten it up as a kid. It was the one day of the year when working at a fish hatchery actually felt cool.

Now he knew it was an endless cycle of hard work, but it was quiet for the most part. The people he'd meet would be one-time visitors whom he didn't have to remember. It had been a quick decision to return, but with every passing moment it felt more and more like the right one. His mother's reply to his glib Can you stand to have your son around full time? I'm a whiz with trout message was an Oh my word. Come home. Can't wait to see you.

Now that he thought about it, her response hadn't exactly been completely affirming. She usually jumped at his offers to visit, but he felt a certain restraint in her answer. Had he overstepped? Another reason he ached to talk to her. *Where are you, Mom?*

Before 5:00 a.m., he saw headlights at the sharp twist in the road that led down the grade to the hatchery. He snatched up the binoculars. It was a van with a logo on the side. The county search and rescue team. Excellent. He'd finally made his case with Sheriff Franco after an entire evening of scouring the property. Maybe it was the six subsequent messages he'd left with police dispatch, but for whatever reason, Franco had decided to send the team he'd borrowed from somewhere. He didn't care where they were from as long as they could find his mother. And he'd pay too, if that's what was required.

With fifty-six acres that butted up to the foothills of Mount Shasta, most of it treacherous and wild, it was impossible to tackle the whole area himself, though he'd spent the entire night trying to do just that. He was cold, sore, his imagination skidding off in all manner of unpleasant directions. The three cups of coffee he'd drunk in the past hour weren't helping him stay calm.

He raced downstairs and onto the porch, looking again through his binoculars. They'd be here in...

There was a loud pop, followed by another. The van headlights shimmied sideways. He gaped. Shots? He tore inside, grabbed the rifle from the hall closet and charged out again, leaping into Big Blue and speeding up the slope with his heart trip-hammering hard enough to convince him it wasn't a nightmare. This was all too real.

The team...had they been hit? Gas pedal to the floor, he covered the quarter mile of twisty road in less than ten minutes, scanning as he went for the source of the shots. He came upon the van, rolled to the shoulder, headlights blazing.

He grabbed the rifle and shoved the door open when a figure loomed into the road between him and the van.

Beau aimed and fingered the trigger. "Stop right there."

The big man with the curly hair was standing with his revolver aimed at Beau's chest. "Lower that gun," he barked in reply. He wore a Security Hounds T-shirt.

"I'm Beau O'Connor. Exiting slowly, keeping my hands where you can see them." Beau did as he promised, blinking in the headlights. "What happened?"

He saw now that globs of red paint were smeared across the van's windshield, dripping onto the ground as if from a grievous wound.

The curly haired man holstered his weapon. "Someone got us with a paintball gun. We almost went over the side. Heard them depart on a motorbike when I started to pursue."

The driver's side window rolled down and a silver-haired woman poked her head out. "We're calling the cops. Let's not stay out here in the open." A dog barked from the interior, followed by another. In the passenger seat, he caught the glimpse of a younger woman with a cell pressed to her ear. A memory whispered past his worry. Hadn't Henny Penny told him her family was going in the search and rescue business? Was she one of the people in the van? Great. Just fabulous.

The man nodded to Beau. "Meet you at the bottom. Keep your eyes open."

Beau let them pass, his rifle handy in case there was another attack. It was unfathomable that anyone would do such a thing. And for what possible reason? As the van drove by, the young woman's gaze riveted to him. She didn't appear panicked, but deeply troubled. He was too. These people who appeared to be strangers and their dogs were coming to help find his mom. Ree had no enemies. Neither did he, that he knew of.

*What about November when someone put you in the hospital?* That was best thought about later.

He rattled down the slope. At the hatchery, he hurried to usher them in. He made sure to close the curtains and lock the door, just in case.

"Hello, Beau," the silver-haired woman said, extending a palm. She was tall, slender, with the upright bearing of a soldier. "We don't usually make such a dramatic arrival."

He nodded and the woman continued after a beat. "Sheriff Franco dispatched us to conduct a search." Again a slight hesitation, as if she were waiting for him to say something. "We're newly contracted with the county to provide search and rescue, so I imagine that took you by surprise."

Surprise? Why would it? His anxiety ballooned. Did he know these people?

She paused again. "You don't mind the dogs in here, do you? They're droolly, but well behaved, even if they are a little shaken up from getting paintballed."

He gestured. "If you can find my mother, you can bring a herd of elephants in here."

The curly-haired man who'd drawn his weapon a few moments before was almost as tall as Beau. He held out his palm. His grip was firm, just shy of aggressive. He cocked a strong chin at Beau, with the same assessing gleam in his eyes as his mother, the similar hesitation. "Now that we've got proper light, you know me, right?"

Know him? *Uh-oh.* "Hey. Good to see you, uh…"

"Chase." He narrowed his eyes and pointed to the big bloodhound at his side. "Dog's Tank."

Beau couldn't think what to say except to grip his hand in an equally solid clasp.

The next person was a slender young woman with a cascade of dark wavy hair, the one who'd been calling the police from the van. She was looking at him in a way that made his breath catch. Was it Henny Penny? Someone else altogether?

"Hi," she said and there was uncertainty. His gut tingled with trepidation. "These are my dogs, Millie and Phil," she added. "I don't think you caught their names earlier."

He'd met them? Was this the same woman with the dogs that had stopped when he'd been driven off the road? He couldn't be sure. His gut tightened, and he wondered again if this county team might actually be the fledgling search and rescuers Henny Penny told him about. He plastered on a charming smile. "Don't know much about dogs, but Phil isn't a bloodhound, is he?"

"No. He's a livestock dog, an Anatolian shepherd. He assists Millie since she's mostly blind."

Well, that had to be one of the coolest things he'd ever heard.

"Of course, we have more dog teams we can bring in if needed," Beth said. "I've got a full house, but you probably already know that."

Did he?

She continued. "Two should be enough to get us started though. I'm going to ask the sheriff to help with security now that we've got some mischief maker with a paintball gun out there."

He led them into the meeting room. They settled awkwardly on the chairs, and again he got the sense he'd messed up. They knew him. The coiled snake in his gut began to writhe.

Chase's expression became downright stony.

"My mother's missing," Beau blurted. "Ree O'Connor." He slid a photo across the table to them, a picture of his mom standing next to him at the Marine Corps graduation ceremony. He wasn't sure which of them displayed the most pride, him in his dress blues or his mom with her arms around his waist. He related his attempts to find her and his worries that she was injured somewhere on the property. "It's fifty-plus acres with the Mesquite Horse Trail to the east, which leads right into a regional open space. Little chance she would have walked out that way. Her vehicle's still in the garage. She has access to the neighbor's pack animals, they own a stable, so I thought it was possible she went for a ride or contracted a local delivery that required a mule, but I called and the owner said she hadn't been by."

Beth started to speak but Chase butted in. "Sorry, but I'm not in the mood to continue this charade. Gotta clear the air here, man. I'm not a beat-around-the-bush kinda guy."

"Chase," Beth said, a warning in her voice. "His mother is missing. That's what we're here for."

"I understand that part, but we aren't going into a situation blind, and if no one else will bring up the obvious, then it falls to me." He stared at Beau. "What's going on with you?"

"What do you mean?"

"Beau, you went to school with my sister Kara, here. Your mom took care of her for months as a matter of fact." He gestured to his family. "You know all of us at least a little because our mothers are friends, but Kara most of all. We're not strangers to you, but you're acting like we are. Why is that?"

Kara. Kara Wolfe. His very own Henny Penny. And this really was the team she'd told him her family was forming. The snake slithered deeper. Now he took a good look at the harnesses most of the dogs wore…emblazoned with the name Security Hounds, which she'd mentioned in passing.

His gut contracted into a tight fist. How could he have missed the clues?

Chase continued. "I get that you're worried and preoccupied, but what gives? Kara told us you had an accident on the road yesterday and you didn't seem to know who she was then either. I can chalk that up to distance, preoccupation, whatever, but we just marched in here up close and personal, which should have jangled some bells for you, right? We're people you've known, at least superficially, for decades, and there's not a flicker of recognition? What's the game? Pretending you don't know us? Is that what this is?"

How could he possibly explain?

Beth arched a brow at her son, but Chase wasn't going to back down. A muscle jumped in his jaw. "My mom's too polite to grill you right now, and so is Kara, but I'm not. And I'm not letting my family work for someone who isn't coming clean either, so you tell me what's going on right now, or we walk."

Kara's face was flamed with pink, and though he wanted to look at Chase, he could not tear his eyes away from her. The woman on the road who'd stopped to help him was Kara. The pulse thrummed in his ears. These people…this family…might as well be strangers he was meeting for the first time. Why hadn't he put it together that Henny Penny's kin would be dispatched to do the search? He wanted to howl with frustration.

"I…" He rubbed a palm over his unshaven chin. How was he going to explain himself?

Every eye in the room, including all three dogs, was riveted on him. "I remember you, who you are, I mean." He gestured helplessly. "But not your faces."

Chase frowned. "What?"

He sought Kara again, his friend since they'd built pinecone towers in the woods. Delicate features with lips perpetually quirked in a smile, glossy hair that framed her heart-shaped face. A beautiful face, and one that was as unfamiliar to him as if they were meeting for the first time. The enormity of his condition engulfed him in a tide of grief. Try as he might, he could not force the truth from his mouth.

"Prosopagnosia," Kara said softly after an endless silence. "Isn't it?"

His misery must have communicated the answer.

"Did it come from the accident?" she said.

He nodded, embarrassment drowning him in inches.

Kara turned to her family. "He's not pretending. He didn't recognize us because he has face blindness."

He forced his head up and met their astonished gazes.

And he didn't recognize a single one of them.

Kara felt a strange combination of relief and sadness. Beau hadn't been pretending not to know her. Prosopagnosia…that's what he had. How tortuous would it be to not remember the faces of the people you cared about? The people who cared about you?

Chase's expression was pure puzzlement. "Er, sorry. I guess I bulldozed into something sensitive here, but I have no idea what we're talking about. What's face blindness?"

"It's relatively rare," Kara said. "I read about it while I was studying for a college physiology class a few years ago. It's a neurological condition where someone can't recognize familiar faces."

Chase heaved out a breath. "I'm sorry. I didn't know."

"No apology necessary." Beau cleared his throat. "I didn't know either until I woke up, and I didn't recognize the lady who was in my hospital room talking to me. Turns out, it was my mother."

"Wow." Chase whistled softly. "So, it's like amnesia? You forgot who she was?"

"Not amnesia. My memory is perfectly fine

about events and all that, but when I see someone, I can't identify if I know them, or if I've met
them before, until I get some sort of clue. Kara
told me you were forming a search team, but with
everything going on, I didn't realize that would
be you all. You didn't use your last name when
you introduced yourselves so…"

What would it feel like to live in a world where
you couldn't tell a friend from everyone else?
Kara's heart squeezed. "Everyone you meet is
a stranger."

"Until they remind me who they are." He
looked at her and offered a smile. "I know you,
Henny Penny. I just needed some help to jump-
start my brain."

Warmth infused her with the use of that childhood nickname. So many lazy summer days
they'd spent together, exploring, until he'd grown
busier with sports and she with her friends and
animals, and eventually Kyle entered the picture.

"People are mostly born with it, but sometimes it's caused by a brain injury." He shrugged.
"Guess you probably all know about that incident in November."

His eyes glimmered with deep emotion she
could not name and she had to force herself to
look away.

He spread his hands. "I'm sorry, Mrs. Wolfe,
Chase, Kara. I know you. Of course I do."

"No harm, no foul," Chase said. "We're new in the SAR game. I should be the one who feels bad for putting you on the spot. I'm not known for my sensitivity. I apologize again. Sorry if I was a jerk about it."

Beau waved off the comment. "You weren't aware. No one is, really. Most people think I'm rude or standoffish. Not important." He slapped his palms on his knees. "My mom. Can you find her?"

"We'll do our best," Kara said. "We'll need a scent article, and it might take a while if she's been all over the property on foot. The dogs will catch her scent easily enough, but they'll need to pick out her most recent trail, which should be the strongest."

"Map of the hatchery grounds?" Chase asked, pointing to the glossy diagram on the bulletin board across from them. "That one current?"

"Yes. The only difference is it doesn't show the two employee residences. John and Sonia Partridge live in one. They're on vacation until Friday. I've left a message and asked them to call if they know anything about where Mom might be. Vince Greyson lives in the other, and he'll be home today, but he didn't have any knowledge about where she might be either. He's trying to get a hold of John and Sonia too. They're camping along a creek somewhere with spotty phone reception."

Beth noted the numbers and names. "All right. Let's get started putting together a plan."

Kara focused on the information and tried to set aside the fact that Beau was darting glances at her. Prosopagnosia. It explained his recent behavior but not why he'd disappeared from the hospital instead of returning her calls. Embarrassment? Shock over the diagnosis?

Had his situation influenced Ree to sell the hatchery? The secret Ree had entrusted her with burned more painfully in her gut but she pushed it aside and ramped up her attention. Every moment that slipped by with a missing person was crucial. If she allowed her thoughts to stray, she could miss a critical detail.

"Two teams for now, Chase and Tank, and Kara with her two dogs. We'll call in Steph and Vance if needed," Beth said. "Beau and I can coordinate from here."

Beau shook his head. "I'm going too."

Kara wasn't surprised. Beau was like Chase in a lot of ways, perpetually in motion, dissatisfied with stillness.

"That's not generally how we do things," Beth said. "We're…"

He stood, ramrod straight like the Marine he was. "Respectfully, ma'am, I'm going to help. I won't interfere, but I have basic medical training. I'm not naive. It's been forty-eight hours. She's in trouble. I need to be sure she's not injured somewhere on the property. Pending that, I'll widen my search."

Kara noted his hard swallow. They all knew if Ree was able, she would have made it home under her own steam, messaged at least. Kara's stomach cinched tighter. This time maybe it would be better if they didn't find their quarry. Perhaps Ree was perfectly safe elsewhere, unaware that efforts were being made to locate her. Possibly the reckless driver, the paintball attack and Beau's earlier accident really were unrelated.

Millie got up and edged close, ever attuned to Kara's moods. Phil planted himself next to Millie. Kara felt strengthened by their proximity. The canine dream team would succeed. She prayed it would be a happy ending.

"All right," Beth said finally. "Beau, you can go with Kara. Radio me every fifteen minutes. I'll liaison with the sheriff."

What would it be like having Beau at her side again? When he'd enlisted, she'd known things would change between them, since he'd expressed his intent to leave small-town life behind, but she'd thought in her naive way that they could somehow maintain the friendship between her, Kyle and Beau. She hadn't understood why her budding romance with his friend created such distance between the three of them. Still, he'd kept in touch after Kyle died, as he moved all over the world. At her urging, they'd enjoyed easy chats and visits when he was in town, up until his last one.

But nothing felt easy about this.

She remained businesslike, checking her radio, fixing a long lead to her bloodhound, and offering both dogs water and a snack while Beau retrieved several items of his mother's.

He provided two choices, one of which was Ree's favorite water bottle that she determinedly drained every day, half full where he'd found it on her tiny desk, the other her favorite coffee mug.

Chase accepted the mug in a plastic bag and readied his dog. "I'll start at the equipment shed. Tank and I will see where the trail leads from there."

Kara zipped her jacket as an impulse struck her. "I've got a different idea. My team will begin at the bird feeder."

"Why?" her mother said in surprise.

"Ree always fed the birds every day at sunup before she started her daily chores. She let me mix up the seeds when I came here after school."

Beau's eyes glimmered and she knew he was remembering too. The hatchery had been a respite for Kara, a place where the rhythms of life were normal when nothing else was. And Ree had been the anchor Kara needed to hold her steady. Every day after school while Beth Wolfe was trying to manage funeral details and the lives of her other children and pack of slobbery bloodhounds, Ree would take her to the hatchery while Beau was at soccer practice or track. They'd grown so close. Maybe that was why Ree had asked her to handle the sale of the hatchery without telling anyone else, even Beau.

And their mutual affection was the reason Kara had accepted. But there was another motivation, she'd come to realize.

It was time for her to stand up on her own and accomplish the goal she'd set for herself before her life spun wildly off track. Her family didn't agree. They wanted to take care of her, shield her as if she was still fragile, but she was stronger than they realized.

Strong enough to watch her fiancé die and survive it.

Brave enough to withstand Beau turning his back on her.

And plenty determined to start her real estate business while working part time to support her family. The sale of the hatchery property for Ree would be her jumping off point. But now the secret-keeping was a source of discomfort.

Kara straightened and pointed to the half-filled jar of seeds on the sill. "Looks like she kept up the practice of filling the feeder."

Beau nodded. "She did—I mean—does. She buys seeds in bulk. No one handles that job but her."

Kara donned a plastic glove to extract the tiny scoop from the jar. "So, if she replenished the feeder yesterday or the day before, we know it's a fresh scent. Millie and Phil can start there." Though she kept her voice calm and controlled, her pulse pounded. What would they find when they followed the trail?

Beth saw them to the door. "Any problems, radio immediately."

Outside, the sky was lightening from black to pewter. Chase and Tank turned toward the equipment shed when a white pickup with O'Connor Hatchery stenciled on the side appeared and a man got out.

He took in the dogs. Phil's nostrils flared in the newcomer's direction. Chase and Tank stopped to watch. Phil squared his shoulders and edged in front of Kara and Millie. "What's going on?" the man boomed.

"Easy, Phil," she murmured. He backed up a tiny bit but remained alert as ever.

Beau, too, was examining the newcomer, the vehicle, the driver's overalls, the cigarettes pok-

ing from the pocket, picking up on cues to identify him, she realized. He cocked his head as if
he were putting the man's unusually deep voice
through an analysis.

"This is Vince Greyson," Beau said finally.
"He works for the hatchery." Beau told him about
the paintball attack.

"Some kids, likely." Vince pulled off his skull-
cap and scrubbed a weathered palm over his
close-shaven hair. Vince looked to be in his early
fifties, but his tanned face spoke of too much
time in the sun. Kara couldn't help scoping out
his hands and boots for any signs of paint. He'd
been close by, after all, though she hadn't the
foggiest idea why he'd do such a thing. But there
were no flecks of paint that she could detect.

"Did you hear from John and Sonia?" Beau
asked.

He chewed his lip. "Not yet, but they'll check
in soon."

"Feed any information you find to Beth Wolfe,"
Beau said. "She's inside, coordinating the search."

His eyes shifted to the dogs again. "The search,"
he echoed. "Is it really necessary? You don't think
she's…?"

"If she's on the property, we'll find her," Kara
said.

Vince marched off to the office without a word.

Find her. That's all they could do, in spite of

the hit-and-run driver and the paintballer. Perhaps they were one and the same? She prayed Ree was still alive. One way or another, they'd put Beau's agony to rest.

# THREE

Beau watched Kara open the plastic bag and let Millie have a deep whiff of the birdseed scoop. Mille's tail wagged, and she was already whirling around, darting past the feeder on its weathered pole toward a gravel path around the parking area. Phil lurched into motion and caught up, his shoulder pressed to Millie's as Kara kept a firm hold on the leash.

Beau's spirits surged. They'd find her. He hurried to catch up. "How did they learn to work together like that?"

"Steph's fiancé picked Phil up at the shelter where he was left after someone walked away from their farm. He was already an efficient livestock guardian. After the initial introductions, I tethered Millie and Phil together for short periods until Phil understood that his job was to protect Millie. Now he does his work without my interference. It's sort of in his DNA to guard things. Once he decided Millie and I were his own personal flock, he was in it to win it."

"Incredible."

"Completely."

"You do this full time now? Work for Security Hounds? I thought you were helping with the books and taking some college classes, last we talked." And before he'd run off. He simply couldn't abide the thought of not being able to recognize her, the humiliation, the explanations, the pity he might see in her. But turning tail had been a cowardly choice.

"I had a chance to train Millie and Phil, so I stepped in. When we got the contract from the county to do search and rescue, Mom needed my help. Or she said she did anyway." She moved ahead another pace and shrugged. "I'm…considering other things, but I'll always be a part of Security Hounds." She paused. "My family was there for me when Kyle got sick, so…"

He looked away. So she'd return the favor. That was Kara to the core. When Kyle passed, the Wolfes had been her lifeline. He'd failed Kara, not caring for her up close and personal the way he'd wanted to, but that involved too many tangled up feelings. He dragged his gaze back to her. "They want you close. I get it."

"They still see me as fragile, but I'm not anymore. It's time to stand on my own."

He'd noticed it too, a new aura of confidence around Kara that intrigued him. What had she learned about herself after losing Kyle? Suddenly he was burning to know the answer, but their pace discouraged conversation as they hustled in the wake of the dogs.

They covered the graveled path and emerged into a rocky hollow full of knee-high green grass where hidden obstacles slowed them. Phil and Millie moved in tandem, carving a path through the stalks as they progressed. Behind, Beau heard the soothing flow of the water and the splash of the fish in the cement raceways. He'd always loved that noise, but now, as they sped farther away, the comforting sound faded, replaced by wind and the unnerving buzz of insects.

The farther they got into the tumbled landscape, the more his agitation increased. There were forces at work he didn't understand, which left him worried his mother's disappearance was sinister. Kara thought so too, obviously. Had the paintballer intended to deter Security Hounds, to prevent them from searching? It wasn't going to work. Kara and her kin were devoted to their mission, and Beau was beyond grateful.

But if there was someone dangerous stalking them...

A breeze chilled his face and seeped through his jacket. He prayed Kara and her family wouldn't be put in any more danger helping him out. He had enough guilt on his conscience where she was concerned.

It wasn't long before they'd left the meadow and joined a route that climbed upward toward the steep, rocky foothills. His mother would have stuck to the path at this point, he was sure, because she wasn't a fan of creatures that slithered, and any shortcuts would provide lots of hidey-holes for snakes.

What about the human kind of predator? He scoured the piles of towering rock, searching for the slightest clue that they were being tracked. There was no sign of anyone. They kept on for a solid half hour until the dogs were panting with exertion and his own forehead was filmed with sweat.

Kara stopped under a sprawling oak tree. "I need to rest them."

Beau's instincts shouted at him to soldier on, but he acquiesced. She set down water and provided snacks for both dogs.

Unable to keep himself still, he paced the wet, leafy litter. As an amphibious assault vehicle crew chief, it had been his responsibility to get infantry troops from ship to shore safely, and that meant a constant threat assessment. Sometimes, even when the ocean was calm and the coast appeared clear of enemy involvement, a tingle in his senses would urge extra caution. That tingle was now coursing through his body. *Your nerves were messed up seven months ago. Can you trust them now?*

"It won't take long," Kara was saying. "But the dogs will push themselves to the point of exhaustion if I don't enforce rest periods."

"Was Millie born blind?" He scanned as he spoke.

"No. She developed progressive retinal atrophy. Her owner looked us up six months ago and asked us to take her." She stroked Millie's head. "I'm so glad we did. She was a good tracker before she lost her vision and she's learning how to work around her limitations."

He wished he had such a positive approach to his own. He shook his head. "Dogs are amazing."

"Yes. They don't know they can't do something, so they aren't afraid to try."

He kept careful watch while the dogs munched. In spite of his unease, there was no indication of any intruder. At least it gave him something to focus on besides his worry and the strange disequilibrium he was experiencing being close to Kara…without Kyle, without his job, without his ability even to recognize her from one day to the next. And why did he have the sense that Kara was withholding something from him? How would he even know?

Rest period over, they continued on.

He watched her from the corner of his eye as she leapt gracefully over muddy places, moving easily. She'd always been light on her feet, a dancer from early on. And with a charisma that enveloped her and everyone else nearby.

He flashed on a memory. She'd been involved in the high school nature preservation club, and he'd been coerced to help with a trash day pickup by her earnest pleading.

"Please, Beau," she'd begged, hazel eyes dancing with a hint of mischief. "If you and Kyle come, way more girls will show up and the jocks too."

He'd folded his arms and crimped a brow at her. "Are you saying you're using us to beef up your numbers at this gig?"

"Yeah," she'd fired back. "Whatcha gonna do about it?"

He'd laughed and done what he always did with Kara, went along with her plans and made sure to convince his water polo team to show too—by promising to buy them pizza afterward. It had cost him fifty bucks, but he hadn't minded. Even in his memory, her face was indistinct, blurred.

But not her voice. And he remembered her fingers, long and elegant and somehow still so delicate, even when she was plying a rake or shovel. The hand that held the leash now was smooth and pale, a freckle just below the right index finger knuckle.

*Memorize it. Bury it deep down in your brain so you never, ever forget her.*

He'd found it was much easier to recognize hands, feet, ears, than complete faces.

With a start, he realized that she'd noticed him staring. She half smiled and flipped the bangs from her forehead, never letting go of her grip on the leash.

"It's lonely," she said. "Isn't it?"

Lonely. The people who knew about his prosopagnosia, a small select group, had offered words like "difficult" or "challenging" to describe his situation. Her assessment arrowed right to his core. It was lonely, pure and simple. The only reason he was able to face the day was that he knew God loved him, no matter what the status of his brain. He clung to that truth with the desperation of a drowning man.

"Yes," he said finally. "People don't like being forgotten, so it's a friendship killer for sure." He hoped she'd understand why he'd ended their friendship too, why he did not want to treat her like a stranger…exactly like he'd done when she'd stopped to help him on the road. Better if she hadn't stopped. Easier on both of them.

But who else would stand by him in spite of the hurt he'd caused?

She was silent a moment, as Phil bumped Millie away from a fissure in the trail. "But the worst part is that you hold yourself back from everyone around you."

He didn't know how she'd ascertained that, but somehow Kara always knew. "I figure that's a better thing to do than hurting people by not remembering them."

"Hiding can hurt people too."

And she was living proof of that. He batted a gnat away from his field of vision.

Millie paused to sniff under a low lying bush. He continued to check the surroundings. Branches shifted, the constant movement hitching his breathing. Plenty of hiding places.

"Lonely, for a guy who was always super social."

She wasn't done with the topic yet? "'Was,' being the operative word. Past tense." When the despair crept higher, he shoved it down. This new life he was building here at the hatchery would be a quiet one, and he'd learn to live with it, to love it, to find purpose again.

She held the leash higher to avoid a muddy patch. "Do you think it's permanent, the prosopagnosia?"

"Good question. Docs like to speculate on that. Bottom line is they've got no idea."

Which left him in a foggy no-man's-land without a career or friends he couldn't recognize, his connections neatly severed in one abrupt moment. A vulture circled slowly overhead, adrift on the icy wind.

She removed a twig that had become tangled in the leash. "Why didn't you return my calls after your attack, Beau?"

The question she'd been wanting to ask for seven months, no doubt. He appreciated the "attack" instead of "your accident," as Sheriff Franco had phrased it, as if he'd somehow fallen down and clubbed himself. "I…it was a lot to process."

"I would have helped."

He didn't know what to say. Her words were flat and toneless, and it brought home the reality that he'd delivered the final blow to their friendship when he'd cut out on her, like a knife sawing through a tender stem. Maybe they'd have ended up simply acquaintances anyway. Too much water under their bridge. "You would have. I know that. I'm sorry."

"Did you leave the Marine Corps?"

He swallowed hard. "No, they left me. Medically retired me. Seems when you can't recognize your officers or anyone else in your unit from one day to the next, you're not fit for duty."

"Oh, Beau."

The softness of her voice, the pity in it, grated on him. "It's okay. Gotta keep moving on." And he knew God had a plan for his life, but it hurt at a level that was almost indescribable. He let his gaze wander into the sprawl of shrubs. "Are you sure the dogs are following the right scent?"

"Yes, but I'll give Millie a refresher." She opened the bag containing the birdseed scoop. Millie sniffed and took off again with Phil at her side. "Did your mother regularly hike up here? I don't remember it being a part of her routine, and she didn't mention it when we talked."

"I didn't know you two stayed in touch."

Kara shrugged. "She gave me a call a few weeks ago."

Interesting. "Years ago she came up with this plan. She'd decided to improve this trail, cut back the trees and fill in the dangerous holes so visitors could climb and get a view of the hatchery and Mount Shasta. Could be she finally decided to do it."

"That would make the property more marketable."

"Marketable?" He arched his brow. The comment struck him as odd until he remembered Kara had wanted to be a real estate agent, once upon a time. "Maybe someday if she chose to sell, but that's not going to be anytime soon."

She skirted a wet patch of ground. "I heard Vince saying to my mom that it's difficult to operate the hatchery with only a few workers."

"It is, but I'm here to help now." He pulled in a deep breath. Time to make things real. "I decided to stay and run the place with Mom."

She faltered, midstride. "Really?"

Why did her face whiten at his statement? Upset that he'd be a fixture in the area? But she'd be too busy with her life and pursuits in Whisper Valley, surely, and they wouldn't cross paths often if he had anything to say about it. "Anyway, she might have made her way up here to review her plan. Fallen, got knocked out." He was grasping at straws. When would she have fallen? Tuesday morning? Evening? It was now Thursday. It hadn't rained any more, but the temps had still dropped into the high forties the night before. The thought of his mother lying there in the elements set his nerves on fire.

Kara tucked a flyaway strand of hair behind her ear. "Did your mom know you were coming back permanently?"

Again he felt that strange sense that she was hiding something. He was about to question her further when Phil cocked his ear to the sky. Beau's senses kicked into high gear as he detected a quiet crunch. The sound of footsteps?

"What?" Kara said.

"I heard something."

She drew Millie to her as Phil began to growl. "Phil did too."

Beau leaned close, whispered in her ear. "It came from behind that crooked tree. I'm going to check." Every nerve in his body was electric.

Kara nodded her understanding, gave Phil the silent command and tapped a finger to Millie's head to convey the same message. Phil stopped growling, but the scruff on his neck rose. He wouldn't let anyone or anything close to her or Millie. Comforting, unless the intruder had a weapon.

Beau turned and crept into the darkest of the shadows, easing his way to the stump, one careful step following another. The damp soil muffled the sound of his boots as he drew closer. The slow creep was excruciating and necessary, like controlling the dust signature of a massive vehicle packed with soldiers. Stay invisible as long as possible. He eased his gun out. There was someone there in the shifting shadows. He could feel it, a presence, human and malignant.

This stalker was going to come clean. Right here and right now.

Kara watched Beau vanish into the dripping branches.

She bit her lip, finger on the radio, ready to call Chase for backup.

What was going on? This was a search and rescue. Who would be hiding? The same person who'd pelted their van with bloodred paint? And tried to run Big Blue off the road?

*Don't jump to conclusions.* It could be an animal they'd heard. Phil too might have reacted to a raccoon or coyote. Every living creature was a possible enemy in Phil's book, a threat to his herd. She thought about Beau's attack on this very same patch of ground all those months ago…a sound that brought him running…an attacker who was never found, an injury that had cost him so much.

"Hold it," Beau shouted.

There was a crunch of branches, the movement of something coming closer.

Breath held, she pressed the radio button, ready to call for help, but before she could speak, a figure dressed in black burst from the shadows, barreling toward her. Slung over his shoulder was a chunky gun, not designed for bullets but for paint pellets. The face was covered by a black balaclava. Man? Woman?

She wanted Phil to stay close, fearful he'd be injured, but the dog charged, barking furiously. The stranger stopped short at the menacing animal, whipped around and bolted, disappearing into the shrubs. Phil pursued for a few yards, then circled back to Millie and Kara.

Beau sprinted into view. His eyes sought hers, and she gave a reassuring nod to show they were all unharmed. Phil barked some more, making it clear where his quarry had headed.

"He disappeared into those bushes," Kara confirmed, urging both dogs into a reluctant sit. Phil tried to comply, but he instantly shot upward again, staring lasers into the foliage, the growl bubbling up.

Gun in hand, Beau sprinted to the overgrown thicket. She could barely control her shaking. The masked person had indeed been watching them. Planning what exactly? Another paintball attack? Beau had no idea who he was tracking.

*Please, Lord. Don't let him get hurt*. She heard the thrum of a motor. A car? No, too high-pitched. Clutching Millie around the neck, Kara waited as the seconds crawled by. Finally, Beau emerged with a look of disgust. "Gone. He had a dirt bike parked near the gully. Took off."

She busied herself with the dogs to prevent him seeing her relief that he was out of danger. The strength of the emotion took her by surprise as she released the dogs from their command. As a search and rescuer, she should be used to such high-stakes moments. Millie immediately whisked her nostrils along the ground while Phil stayed close. "I'll radio Chase and Mom."

He exhaled. "Good. I'm pretty sure he's gone, but…"

She offered a weak smile. "There's no harm

in hoping for the best as long as you're prepared for the worst."

He smiled back, the first true grin she'd seen from him since he'd landed in her life again. He looked like the Beau she remembered from their high school days, warm, slightly goofy, positive. "That's my mom's old saying."

"I know."

Their connection lasted a moment before she relayed the information and Chase rerouted toward their location. "But we're continuing on the search."

"Negative," Chase barked. "Hold in place until I get there."

"We're close to finding Ree. The dogs can feel it. We'll keep you apprised." She clicked off. Her brother would have plenty to say to her later. Right now, she felt as tense as her bloodhound. Phil was returned to his normal level of wariness, but Millie was tugging hard in her need to track her target. She rechecked Millie's harness. "That had to be the same person who fired at our van."

Beau nodded.

Crashes. Paint pellets. Stalkers. Ree's disappearance. "There are an awful lot of things going wrong since you arrived back in town."

He twitched. "You think I'm the target?"

"Don't you?"

He was quiet for a minute. "Pretty clear that

someone doesn't want me around, or anyone coming to help me."

"Who would hate you that much?"

He didn't answer as they lurched into motion.

It wasn't the right moment to discuss it, but she couldn't help herself. "What if it's connected to what happened in November? You were about to stumble upon something, or someone, and they attacked you. Maybe they're back again."

"Why though?"

She had no answer, not even a theory. Who was this paintball stalker? And what had he intended to do if Beau hadn't detected him? Her gut told her it was all related. But how? And why?

Those questions would have to wait. Ree needed them now.

The dogs had sped up, Millie's nose quivering as she pulled at the leash. Phil kept to the outside of the trail, the side that dropped away to a steep wooded slope. Had Beau's mom fallen over the edge? Been pushed? Kara's body prickled with gooseflesh. Millie led the pack around a sharp turn. Her snuffling turned into a long, throaty howl that made Kara's jaw clench.

They were running now. Was Ree up ahead?

The tension was like an electric current sizzling through Millie, her shoulders steeled, tail erect. They catapulted around a turn and Kara slipped on the wet soil.

Millie was ninety pounds of determination, and it took all Kara's strength and a prod from Phil to tug the bloodhound to a stop. Beau narrowly avoided crashing into them.

She looked at him, her mouth held tight as she pointed to the snow-dotted slope that fell away from the trail.

He scanned frantically. There was no sign of his mother. "Where is she?"

Millie whined and tugged on the leash.

He hardly heard her until she gripped his arm. "What?"

"Look there."

He followed her gesture and saw the disturbed grass, the flattened section where someone had walked.

"Millie's indicating she left the trail and went that way, toward the rocks." Why would she trek over such rough terrain? It didn't make sense if she was examining the trail for possible improvements.

Beau tore ahead of them, pounding down the slope.

The trampled area curved, turned, edged off toward the tumbled ridge of granite boulders. There was a narrow gap there that led down into the lower meadow. Kara took a few precious moments to alert Chase before she allowed Millie and Phil to continue. The going was steep, crescents of snow concealing mushy patches underneath which even Phil could not keep Millie from sinking into. The dogs scrambled and plunged their way forward.

They caught up with Beau, Kara's lungs burning until suddenly Millie stopped. Kara scanned for broken grass, a depression in the ground, but she saw nothing except moss-covered rocks. Millie brought her head up, wandering in circles as she sifted through the new information. What had happened? How had they lost the scent?

"Mom! Where are you?" The wind twirled Beau's words away.

"Beau, let Millie do her job. She needs a minute."

He nodded, panting and stepped aside.

Kara let the leash out, refreshed the scent again, and Millie flapped her ears, then zoomed to the rocks, inhaling deeply along the periphery. Had Ree taken a shortcut through the notch to the lower pasture? Why would she?

Beau suddenly twisted, looking at something. She tried to follow his gaze.

A disturbed animal or bird? Stone still, he scanned the rock pile and the cliff face above. She could not see anything to cause alarm, but her heart pounded anyway. Paintball guy returning?

Phil's attention darted to the rocks now too. Movement? Beau's mom?

Kara's elation turned to disbelief as she saw the sizzle of light streak through the air. Beau sprinted, grabbed Kara with one hand and Millie's leash with the other.

"Run," he urged, herding them in front of him and into the trees. Phil growled, but at least he was moving in a safe direction.

The dynamite arced a trail of sparks, disappearing into a crevice between a cluster of rocks above. All that granite perched above. Let loose, it would crush them like twigs.

"Faster," he said. "We have to get to—"

But his words were lost in a massive boom.

# FOUR

Kara felt a shove to her lower back. The ground around her reverberated with the crash of falling rocks. Rough ground scraped her palms as she landed hard between two pine trees. Millie yelped somewhere, but Kara was too dizzied to track her. She felt the silky touch of an ear, a wet nose and hauled Millie close, the dog's sides heaving against her own.

Bits of rocks and leaves rained from the sky, larger hunks slamming down. None of it hit her. It was deflected by something—no, someone—she realized.

Beau's body was braced over hers, his palms planted in the pine needles, shielding her. She could feel the corded muscles in his forearms, the thuds as he was struck by the falling debris. He didn't cry out, or maybe she couldn't hear him over the tumult. Dust assaulted her eyes and infiltrated her nose.

Slowly the onslaught lessened and stilled, until

she could discern only her own harsh breathing and the panting of her two dogs since Phil had burrowed his way into her proximity.

Millie wriggled against her stomach, turning to slather her chin with a wet tongue. Phil added his slobbery greeting. Beau stirred and knelt next to her as she sat up with a lap full of dogs.

His eyes shone with concern as he peered around Phil's bulk. "You okay?"

"Yes," she said. "Are you?"

He nodded.

Phil circled her and Millie, legs stiff and scruff raised. Not injured that she could tell from a quick glance.

"Ready," she commanded. They immediately scrambled to sit shoulder to shoulder, the position she'd taught them when she first started training them as a team. Both were alert and enthusiastic, cooperative as she kneeled and performed a quick exam.

She sighed in relief. No blood. No painful spots where she'd skimmed her fingers. The knot in her stomach eased.

"They're okay?" Beau's forehead was streaked with dirt, and there was a bloody scrape showing through the torn elbow of his jacket, but he too appeared in one piece.

"I think we're all intact." *Thank you, Lord.* She brushed debris from her clothing. "I—"

A loaf-sized boulder rolled loose from the pile and tumbled within a few yards of them.

Phil immediately inserted himself between the humans and the foe, charging the stony intruder and barking so loud the noise pierced right through her ear drum. Beau grabbed her shoulder, ready to pull her back, but the rock changed direction and flopped to a halt.

Beau exhaled.

Phil continued to circle the rock as if it might sprout legs and come after them.

Kara wondered how many other stones were out there waiting to roll loose. Or might they have had more help? Was someone still hiding out, trying to bury them alive? She dismissed the sinister thought. Phil wasn't alerting that there was another person lingering in the woods or in one of a million hiding spots on the cliff. Then again, Phil was a livestock guardian, not a trained detection animal, but he was the most protective dog she'd ever worked with.

When Phil was certain the rock wasn't posing an additional threat, he returned to his charges, ears flicking. Beau looked from Phil to the tree line. "Does he hear something we can't?"

"I don't think so. He's on threat alert, but he's confused. He's used to coyotes and wolves, not rock falls."

Phil contented himself with silent reconnaissance. He rejoined Millie, who tipped her nose to the sky too, perhaps to try and make sense of what had happened.

And what *had* actually gone down in the last few minutes? Kara's senses still rattled and buzzed, expecting more catastrophe to rain down on them. One minute they'd been close to finding Ree and the next...

Beau urged them a few paces deeper into the trees. "Stay here, okay?"

"Where are you going?"

"Not far. Promise."

She didn't argue, her breath still coming in shallow gasps. The three of them watched as he jogged quietly toward the slide area. Stealth was his aim, she realized. He made hardly any noise as he ran. The rockfall had obviously been caused by some sort of explosion. And Beau was behaving as if he believed whoever had caused it was still out there, no matter what Phil indicated. She pulled her zipper up tighter. The rattling leaves echoed like whispering voices. The O'Connor property was sprawling, wild, and it had never felt so cut off from the rest of the world.

If someone really had caused the rockfall, they had to have been tracking her, Beau and the dogs as they searched. It had to be the person with the paintball gun. Maybe they were still watching at that very moment from some concealed crevice. Was Beau in grave danger, prowling around now?

She rubbed Millie's ears. The dog had been closing in on a scent before the slide. No question they'd been close to finding Ree. Now a massive cascade of rocks and earth covered the trail, obliterating any clues. There would be no easy or quick way to bypass the rubble. The only chance was to hike to the location from the other side of the blockage. A fine dusting of grit drifted through the air as she groped for her radio.

"What happened? Landslide?" her mother demanded. "Chase is almost to you. Injuries? Should I dispatch first aid?"

She reassured her mother that all four of them were unharmed.

Beth was a retired Air Force captain, so her tone was collected, all business, but Kara detected the fear underneath. "I'll need a full status report, pronto, after I contact the sheriff."

"Beau will be able to fill in some details, but we can't continue the search from this direction. The slide has completely blocked the trail." She paused. "I believe that was the intent, Mom. The landslide wasn't an accident."

Her mother went quiet. "The intruder's still out there. You need to retreat for now."

"We're okay. Beau's checking the area. We have to figure out how to continue the search."

Beau reappeared as they were discussing options.

"Whoever did it is gone." A vein jumped in his jaw.

"Report?" her mother snapped over the radio.

Kara handed the device to Beau.

"Mrs. Wolfe…" he started.

"It's Beth. I want to hear it all right now. You and Kara have reason to believe this was an intentional act by the person you chased away earlier?"

"Affirmative. There was movement from the rocks above us where we were searching. I got only a glimpse. The person lobbed a stick of dynamite from the rock pile and caused a slide. They knew where to let it loose, which means they'd been tracking us and calculating the right time to cause the slide."

Kara's mouth went dry.

There was a beat of silence from her mother. "Are you and the dogs in a safe position now?"

"Yes, ma'am. I suspect he or she has taken off on the motorbike."

"In case they haven't…"

"I'm monitoring, ma'am, and I'm armed."

All Kara's brothers and her sister carried weapons, since they were former police or military. Kara was the oddball who didn't, and she knew her siblings weren't overly confident in her

ability to protect herself. Maybe they were right.
If Beau hadn't reacted as quickly as he did… She
rested her hand on Phil's white fuzz. She'd trust
her safety to Phil any day of the week, but even
he couldn't protect against a stalker who might
have tried to kill them. Phil was clearly going to
give it his all. He and Beau looked equally tense,
all tight muscles and coiled energy.

*Don't get too comfortable having them look
out for you. You can take care of yourself now,
remember?*

"Chase will be there any minute to escort you
all down. Hold in place until he arrives," her
mother said.

"Yes, ma'am." Beau handed Kara the radio,
and they remained in the shelter of the dripping
branches.

Kara brushed the mess from her jeans.

Beau's gaze roved the rock pile, calculating,
assessing. "She could be under there. Or lying
on the other side."

Kara took his hand and squeezed. She'd forgotten how long his fingers were, overlapping
hers by inches. "We'll get to her. Find a way to
bypass and continue the search." But her stomach
twisted when she gazed out on the wheel-sized
rocks that had been blasted loose from the mountain and rolled across the path. If Beau hadn't
noticed the threat and pushed her out of the way,

she and the dogs would have been crushed. So much for taking care of herself. She shoved away the thought.

But why would someone do such a thing? For what purpose? To prevent them from finding Ree? Was she the target or Beau?

Beau scanned with the binoculars for the twenty minutes it took until Chase hustled into view, Tank loping at his side.

Phil barked at Tank, as he did at every living thing that came close to herself or Millie, but Chase's burly bloodhound was unperturbed. Not much got under Tank's skin. He was the epitome of the word "chill." The same could not be said of her brother. Chase was a spinning top at the best of times, which this clearly wasn't.

Surreptitiously, she glanced at Beau. What did he see? she wondered. Would he recognize Chase or think him a stranger? No, she decided. He'd consider context, Chase's identifying characteristics, his curly hair, the dog with a search and rescue vest. What a lot of details to take into account instead of the instantaneous recognition most people enjoyed. Recognition was a gift from God she'd never valued properly before.

"Chase." Beau spoke with a tinge of emphasis that made her suspect he was proving to her brother that he knew exactly who he was.

Chase stopped and looked almost accusingly

at Beau. "What happened? Mom told me only the bare bones."

Beau repeated the report he'd just given to her mother. "There's more at play here than we knew."

"Clearly." Chase frowned. "And if you'd stayed in place like I told you…"

Kara held up a hand. "Stop, Chase. This isn't the time."

Her brother exhaled, loud and slow. "Okay. New plan. We go back to camp and find a work-around to the blockage. Not enough light to stage a new search today. First thing tomorrow."

"That's not acceptable. I have to look for my mother. Millie followed the scent and reacted." Beau looked at her and she nodded her assurance. "Mom has to be here."

"Not arguing that. If the dogs say it's true, it is. But it's important we don't add to the victim list, and I'd be saying that even if my sister wasn't one of the participants." Chase's chin went up. "I'm sorry. The search is suspended for now."

Beau did not raise his voice—he'd always been soft spoken—but she saw the crimp in his mouth, the slight lift to the shoulders. She'd only seen him lose control of his temper once.

She flashed back to Beau in that moment, a high school senior in his water polo sweatshirt and jeans, uneven haircut courtesy of his mother.

He'd seen that their neighbors, Natalie and Rocklin Clark, had acquired a dog that Rocklin had chained in the yard, against the wishes of his wife, to scare off a mountain lion he'd spotted in the area. Iggy was a gentle giant with a thick fur coat who wanted nothing more than affection, but the dog wasn't permitted in the house and was rarely released from his chain.

Beau had spoken to Rocklin, offered to walk Iggy, even adopt him, but no matter how much he and Rocklin's wife had pleaded, the dog remained chained to the tree all through that blazing summer. When winter hit, Beau had had enough. She'd been there, with Beau's best friend Kyle, the three of them working on ideas for the upcoming school winter festival. When the first snowflakes landed, Beau had watched them drift for a moment before he'd suddenly leapt to his feet and slammed out the back door, Kara and Kyle following.

Beau had pounded on the door. Rocklin answered.

"You cannot leave that animal out here with no doghouse, Mr. Clark. He's freezing. His ears are frostbitten."

Rocklin arched a thick brow at Beau, folding his arms across his stocky chest. "Dog's my property," he said from the doorway. "I'll do what I like with him. Nobody interferes with my business."

Beau had gotten progressively more furious until Kara and Kyle had to drag him back to the hatchery, where he'd immediately driven into town and come as close to shouting as she'd ever heard him while making a complaint to the sheriff.

Animal control investigated. Rocklin was cited, fined and put on notice.

Rocklin retaliated by dumping the dog in a shelter. Beau had promptly adopted him, refused money from Kyle and Kara, who'd wanted to help. Instead, he'd worked extra shifts in town at the pizzeria to afford the veterinary treatments to heal Iggy's frost-damaged skin. Iggy had remained his devoted companion until he passed before Beau enlisted.

Beau had refused ever to discuss the incident again.

She focused on the standoff between Beau and her brother.

Beau stood wire taut, a few inches taller than Chase, whose expression read, *I'm not backing down. Deal with it.*

Chase shook his head. "I understand your frustration, I really do, but we can't continue to search right now. The area is unstable for the dogs and handlers, and there's a threat out there, obviously."

"Not we. Me. I'm not asking anyone to put themselves at risk." Beau's mouth firmed into a tight line. "Take Kara and the dogs. I'll bypass the slide. Circle back where Millie alerted if I can. I'll handle it. Alone."

"You're not going to—" Chase started.

"You'd do the same." The four words cut through Chase's diatribe. The men looked unblinkingly at each other.

Chase offered a tiny nod. "Yes, I would." Respect was silently exchanged between the two.

Kara knew they were both right. And she also knew Beau had no one. He'd hurt her in the recent past, for sure, but she could never stand to see someone fighting a battle alone. His mother was important to her too. Again she felt the twinge of guilt. It was much easier to stomach keeping a secret from Beau when he wasn't standing right next to her.

"I'll put up the drone. We have one with a low-light camera," Chase said. "Make sure Paintball Dude isn't hanging around."

"All right." Beau gathered his pack.

She took a breath. "We're not quitting until we find her." She laid a hand on Beau's arm. He looked at her fingers, studying them for a long moment. When he spoke, he did not meet her gaze.

"Your brother's right. I'm going solo tonight," he said to his boots. "It's not safe here. Sheriff's on his way. I have a lot of ground to cover. I'll check in with you regularly." He turned and began to pick his way through the detritus around the trail the attack had obliterated.

And that was what it had been, she reminded herself. Not an accident. A direct attack.

Had it been caused by someone who didn't want them to find Ree? Someone responsible for her disappearance? Or the reckless driver who'd driven Beau and Big Blue off the road? The paintball attacker? She flashed for a moment on Rocklin Clark's threat all those years ago.

*Nobody interferes with my business.* Beau had made an enemy of Rocklin at that moment. But that happened a decade prior. Had he nursed some kind of bizarre grudge against Beau or his mother? But what would be the point?

Beau was moving steadily away, nimble in spite of his big size. She made up her mind. She handed Millie's leash to her astonished brother. Phil followed Millie, though he shot a confused glance at her.

"I'm going to help him look."

Chase's eyebrows zinged upward. "No way, Kara. I'm not letting you do that."

Before the experience of Kyle's illness and death, she would have likely acquiesced. Never one to make waves, she had found it was easier to allow people to make decisions for her, to protect her in the way they felt was best. But something had changed in her psyche as she'd stepped up for her fiancé in ways she never would have imagined. And now she couldn't retreat from the new person she'd become and allow others, even her brother, to be in charge of her decisions. She touched Chase's shoulder and softened her words with a smile. "I'm not asking your permission."

"Kara…"

She didn't wait for him to finish, turning away and talking over her shoulder. "I love you, Chase, and I'll be careful, for sure. The dogs need to warm up back in the office and have treats. Water too. Radio me with drone info." Her strides quickened as she skirted the piles of rubble to catch up with Beau. Phil barked, once. She could practically feel Chase fuming.

Beau wouldn't want her making the journey any more than her brother, but Beau had been run off the road, attacked on the trail, and his mother was missing.

And whatever had happened on the property the year before had stripped him of something he desperately needed.

She wasn't going to let him face it all alone.

Beau was locked into finding the quickest way to circumvent the ground failure. The landscape butting up to the blasted trail was a mess of mucky snow-spattered soil and thick clusters of trees. In order to steer clear of the debris, he'd have to hike around the glade, bypass it and rejoin the trail farther up. Then what? Climb back down the trail from the overlook and try to find the spot the dogs had fixed on before the slide?

He didn't hear Kara's approach until she spoke. "North of here is the overlook, isn't it?"

He spun around, his banged-up shoulder throbbing. There she was, curly hair, slender frame in the too big Security Hounds vest, and those graceful legs, as if she'd stepped right out of his memories. How could she possibly look the same as she had in high school? There had always been plenty of boys in line to date her, boys who didn't smell like fish and drive third-hand trucks with names. Kyle for example. A good man. A great friend. *You snooze, you lose.* He'd contented himself with friendship, even after they'd graduated and Kyle proposed to the object of Beau's long-standing crush. He kept his tone calm and controlled. "Kara, you have to go back with Chase."

She gave him a smile, her irises shifting from blue to green in the fading light. He remembered those iridescent eyes, but not the steel he now saw nestled deep.

"Don't waste time, Beau. Chase doesn't get to boss me and neither do you. But while we're stopped…" She offered him a water bottle. "Hydration, right?"

He didn't accept the water. No way was she going to charm herself into taking risks for him, even if she was kind of adorable with the smattering of freckles on her nose and the elfin smile that he was certain he couldn't possibly ever forget.

*Take care of business, Marine.* Sure he'd never been able to say no to her when they were kids, but this was different, and he didn't care how determined she was. He folded his arms. "I'm not moving from this spot until you leave."

"Well, that's going to be awkward for you then." With a grin, she stuck the water bottle in his jacket pocket and simply bypassed him, leaving him standing there with his mouth open.

"Eventually when we rejoin the trail, it leads to the overlook, right?" she tossed over her shoulder. "From there we can get a view of the slide, and what else? This path hadn't been cleared when I used to hang out here with your mom, so you'll have to fill me in."

He got himself together and hurried around her for another try. Calm voice. Relaxed body language, posture certain and commanding, like he'd been as a crew chief for a twenty-one-ton armored assault vehicle. Surely he could manage one small, sweet woman. "I appreciate what you're trying to do, truly, but it's a no-go. Turn around and head down. Please." He threw in the "please" to show it was a request instead of a command, even though it wasn't. "I'll report when I can."

She tipped that delicate chin up at him, and her teasing morphed into something unyielding, stripping her smile away. Suddenly she was not the same Kara Wolfe he'd collected pinecones with during her wreath-making phase, the easygoing young woman who got along with everyone. His pulse ticked up a notch.

"You think you have a right to tell me what I can or cannot do, Beau? After you ignored me when you were hospitalized? Refused to even communicate with me? Now suddenly you're my boss? I don't think so."

Her pain burned into him like a torch. He'd been so lost in his own sadness, he hadn't considered hers, the terrible wound he'd inflicted by walking away on top of the one she'd already endured losing Kyle. He'd been so focused on what had happened to his brain, his world. A bomb had detonated everything familiar, and it had taken months for him to be able to care for himself. Or maybe it had required that long for his spine to regrow. "I apologize for leaving town without telling you. I didn't mean to hurt you."

"Well, you did, Beau. I know you had your reasons, but you shut me out, just like…"

Just like when she'd begun dating his best friend Kyle right before their high school graduation. Couldn't blame her for choosing him. He was an exceptional man, and he'd taken Kara to the final dance when Beau dithered around too long to ask her himself. After graduation, Kara and Kyle's relationship had grown and flourished, and it hadn't surprised Beau when Kyle popped the question on Kara's twenty-fourth birthday.

It was easy to go his own way after graduation, miss the reunions, politely decline the wedding invitation since he was serving in Germany. His work allowed him to dismiss thoughts of his high school crush and his buddy. They'd have a happy life together, and Kyle was a much better match for Kara than Beau, obviously. Maintaining a friendship with them was too awkward, and he didn't know how to navigate it, so he'd chosen not to. Another type of walking away.

But one eight-letter word four years before had changed everything.

Leukemia.

Kara's voice was tentative and tortured in her voicemail message to him.

*Beau, I know you're not great at staying in*

*touch, but I thought you should know Kyle has an aggressive form of leukemia. Call me. Please.*

He'd called, tried to support his friends from a distance and when he'd returned home for visits, but it was so completely awkward with him and Kara and Kyle that he'd bungled it all. Honestly, he'd probably added more confusion to the situation than solace.

"You're gonna get through this, buddy. Kara needs you."

Kyle had smiled. "Doing my best, Beau."

When Kyle passed four months after diagnosis, Beau committed to help Kara if he could, wrote down a contact schedule and stuck to it. Checking in with her regularly to see if he could assist in any way, but the closer they got, the weirder he felt about it.

*What do you need, Henny Penny? What can I do?* He'd meant from a safe distance, through phone calls, emails, etcetera.

"I could really use a friend. Someone who knew Kyle like I did. Would you have coffee with me when you're home on leave?"

With trepidation, he had. And they'd somehow constructed an easy friendship, nothing too deep, not sharing too much, or getting too close, though it was difficult. He'd found himself absolutely delighted to have Kara back in his life.

Until he'd blown that by running from the hospital like a rabbit fleeing its own shadow.

Even with Kyle gone for years, Beau still felt his presence in the air between them.

"I'm sorry, Kara. I... I wasn't the kind of friend you needed when Kyle died."

She blinked hard and looked away. "That's in the past, isn't it?"

Not far enough.

He realized he'd been standing there mutely while she waited for some kind of a response. All he could manage was a nod of the head.

Her mouth pinched into a little bow of disappointment. "I thought we'd finally come to the place where we could be friends again."

He stared at her, desperately seeking to ingrain every last detail of her lovely face into his brain. *How can I be friends with a person I won't know tomorrow? The woman who was supposed to be married to my best friend? Someone who makes me feel things...*

She didn't understand. Never would. Because she was fearless about expressing her emotions, and he'd rather bury his under a mountain of sand. While he was groping around for another way to prevent her from accompanying him, she shook her head and pointed past him.

"Never mind. Let's work on a plan to get the dogs up here. When we reach the overlook, what are we going to see? A view of the slide from the north, the hatchery and what else?" Without waiting for him to answer, she brushed by again, stepping gracefully over a fallen log.

"Kara..." Obviously, he could argue himself into laryngitis and she was still coming along. *You're not going to win this one unless you intend to throw her over your shoulder and carry her back to the office.* He zipped his jacket too forcefully and caught his chin in the process. *Now you can worry about both Mom and Kara. Awesome.* "From the overlook, you can see Mount Shasta and the foothills and the entire hatchery down below. The view's spectacular, which is why Mom wanted to improve the trail as an added attraction for guests." He came alongside her. "All I need is some kind of clue to help me find her."

*And to keep you out of harm's way.*

"All right then. We know where we need to go." She looped her arm through his, and his heart thudded against his ribs. He thought of Kyle, elbows linked with Kara as they walked to take their seats in the stands to attend his graduation from boot camp. Their coupledom simultaneously made him happy and sad.

"First whiff of danger and you take cover, okay?"

"Yes, sir," she said. "Once we get a good look,

we'll choose a way to get the dogs up here safely, and we'll find her. It's what we do."

The objective exactly, but there was no way she should be risking everything to come with him. He tried to work out another approach to dissuade her, but he came up with nothing.

The purr of a drone caught their attention before the small machine whirred across the horizon. Chase reported on the radio.

"No unfriendlies spotted, but there's plenty of places where—"

"Got it," Kara said. "We'll stay alert."

Beau chuckled as she put the radio back in her pocket. "I think your brother had more to say."

"It's best to keep the conversation short when Chase is stewing."

He suspected there would be a subsequent discussion later.

They kept as much to the open spaces as they could, but eventually the thick shrubbery and lush forest closed in. The birds flicked through the branches and sent his nerves tumbling. They again spotted the Security Hounds drone dipping and circling as Chase continued his eye in the sky.

It wasn't likely that they'd been tracked, since they'd had to trek so far away from the trail, over scoured slopes with no place for concealment, but the drone support was reassuring. Sirens down below indicated the arrival of the sheriff, which would be a further deterrent, and Beau stopped every half mile to scan their surroundings in all directions.

"Paintball Guy has to be a local."

She nodded. "I thought so too. Someone who's familiar with the area. How well do you know the hatchery employees?"

"I've known Vince for a long time, the Partridges not so much because they're pretty new, a little over a year on the property."

"What do you think of Vince?"

"Never had a problem with him."

"Why do I hear hesitation?"

"Good worker and my mom trusts him."

"But you don't?"

"He's okay. Not a warm fuzzy guy, but neither am I, maybe. He's honest and hardworking, ethical, far as I'm aware."

"Can you think of anyone else who knows the land and could have it in for you?" Kara asked. Her cheeks were two pink roses from the exertion. At least the strenuous climbing kept them warm.

"No one that I can think of."

Chase confirmed that the sheriff was dispatching personnel to the slide area.

Her eyebrow arched. "Something tells me the sheriff's arrival is a mixed bag for you."

"Glad the cops are involved. That cop, in particular, thinks there's something sketchy about me. He's right, I guess, since when I reported my mom missing I didn't recognize him as the one who handled the prior attack on the property." He shrugged. "Embarrassing, to say the least."

"Why don't you tell him?" she said quietly. "About your diagnosis?"

"Thinking of having it printed on a T-shirt," he joked. "I don't recognize you. Nothing personal."

His quip only made her frown, so he plowed on, eager to change the subject. "If the cops can help, they're more than welcome. Even Franco."

"People can be more understanding than you think."

A vein pulsed in his jaw. "Understanding is a close neighbor of pity, and I don't need that from anyone."

"Is that why you left without telling me? You were afraid I'd pity you?"

"You went through enough with Kyle. Didn't need another case, did you?"

She recoiled and he grabbed her hand, face pained. "I'm sorry. I know he wasn't a case. I'm on the ragged edge and I can't believe I said that."

She gripped his fingers. "It's okay."

But it wasn't, and he resolved to keep a tighter rein on his mouth.

They walked in silence around a sharp bend

and he kicked a pinecone aside. It sailed over the edge down onto a hollow where brilliant green grass shone through small patches of snow.

"Who would want to hurt your mother?"

"Great question. I can't think of anyone."

"Does she get along with her neighbor? The stable owner? I sort of remember they did, but things change sometimes."

He raised a brow. "Natalie Clark? Sure. Natalie's real generous about allowing Mom to ride anytime she wants to. Never charges. She let me do the same when I was a kid. I liked her daughter Fallon, though she was older and left for college when I was in eighth grade. Mom watches the property when Natalie needs to travel, and Vince and John help with the horses if she's away."

"But her husband, Rocklin, wasn't your biggest fan."

"Yeah. Not my favorite person and he undoubtedly feels the same. I never had anything to do with him after I adopted Iggy. He's moved someplace else. Mom said he took up with another woman and left Natalie high and dry." He kicked aside another ravaged pinecone. "Not surprised. A guy who could care less about his dog probably treated his wife just about as well. Slim chance he had anything to do with the slide."

"Chase says you always have to consider your enemies might look like perfectly regular people, like neighbors even, and consider what they have to gain."

"Chase is right, and Rocklin would certainly fall into the enemy camp if he was around, but I don't see the motive."

"So, what's your theory?"

"Me? Aside from Rocklin, I can't figure out who would want to hurt me or my mother."

"The person who attacked you might be back."

"Possibly it's not connected." But was it likely he'd experienced a second random act of violence while visiting Pine Bluff? A third, in fact, if they counted the hit-and-run. His mind drifted to the past, that Thanksgiving night when he'd gone out to walk off his mom's turkey dinner. He could hear his boots sticking slightly to the muddy ground, the rustling of the leaves. The husky male voice, a shout, a gleam of a yellow sleeve, the sounds of a scuffle...his own feet running.

"Who's there?" he'd yelled.

Then an explosion of pain to his skull and the ground rising to meet him. He'd never seen his attacker, but whoever had hit him was an enemy for sure. Could that enemy have returned and made his mother disappear?

Kara's foot slipped and he reached out to steady her.

If he did have such a determined foe, Kara was in danger just being near him.

# FIVE

With effort, Kara matched Beau's long strides. Clearly, he didn't want to revisit the past, but she felt even more strongly that it held the key to what was unfolding in the present. "After your attack in November, did you suspect anyone? Rocklin? Did it sound like his voice you heard arguing?"

"One of the voices might have been his, but I can't be sure. Franco asked me the same question about enemies, and Rocklin was my first thought, actually. I told the cops that. He was the logical choice, since he lived close and obviously hated me, but Natalie explained he'd already left her a couple of days before. Packed a suitcase and took off. Cops called his cell after my attack. He spoke to them from a hotel in Copper Top, where he was staying until his flight to Italy. Class act, leaving Natalie like that."

She felt deflated. So much for keen detective work. "All right. If it wasn't Rocklin, could one of your mom's employees have been involved that night? You said they were male voices you heard, so maybe John or Vince?"

He shook his head. "Vince has been with Mom for twelve years at least. He was a friend of my dad's. Came on full time when Dad had to slow down due to heart disease. He cares about my mom. I don't believe he'd be a threat to me, because it would hurt her."

"How about John Partridge? When did he and Sonia move here?"

"Not sure the exact date, but it wasn't until after that night. Only Vince lived on the property at that point. They're locals, or at least John is. They didn't come to live here until sometime in January, I think because Mom heard John's trailer was wrecked in a storm."

Kara considered. "We'll keep them all on the suspect list anyway. Just because they didn't live here at the time, they're all connected to you and your mom in some way."

Beau scrubbed a palm across the back of his neck. "How did we get to having a suspect list? Until a few hours ago, I figured Mom had fallen and hurt herself."

"That might still be the case, but..." She trailed off. "If it wasn't someone connected with the hatchery when you were struck, then some random stranger just happened to arrive that night?"

"That'd be random all right. We're out in the boondocks. Visitors constantly get lost on their way here and call us for directions."

The wind toyed with her ponytail. "Like you said, it's possible that whatever is happening now has nothing to do with the past."

"More like probable."

She heard her own doubt echoed in his tone. She didn't believe the incidents were unrelated. The hatchery, the quiet surroundings, would not invite random acts of violence. There was something tying the situations together, or someone. If it wasn't Vince, John and Sonia or the neighbors…then who? And why?

Beau shot her a quick glance. "I…appreciate that you believed me about the attack. Certainly there was no proof found to back me up. Sheriff Franco asked me repeatedly if I'd been drinking or taking meds." He rolled his eyes. "Nothing stronger than my mom's tea. That's enough to keep me up for a week straight."

She giggled. Ree brewed her own potent blend from the leaves and herbs in her garden. "Sure is. I used to have a glass in the morning during Pioneer Day and that would keep me going until the crowds dispersed." She noticed he went quiet. "I haven't been to the celebration since Kyle died." Saying his name aloud with Beau felt simultaneously wrong and right.

That long-ago spring day felt like part of a whole separate life, and she'd been a completely different person, a tender twenty-five-year-old. They'd both been on break from school, so she'd offered to help Ree lead tours and prepare the grounds. Kyle met her there on a perfect sunny afternoon, and they'd had a picnic on the hatchery grounds, feasting on berry pie and homemade vanilla ice cream and enjoying the music. Ree bustled and beamed, so proud to greet them. Kyle had been unusually tired, actually falling asleep during the concert. He explained it away as too many late nights studying for his entrance exams to dental school. He would graduate college in a matter of weeks and start his postgrad work. Understandable that he'd be tired, thin from grabbing snacks on the go, worn down. And the massive nosebleed, which had thoroughly embarrassed him, had to be the result of the dry air in the closet-sized apartment he'd rented. All the explanations were plausible, but something about his pallor set off a silent alarm inside her.

Would the outcome have been different if she'd listened to her instincts and insisted he go to the doctor that very day? Driven him there herself before he returned to his final few weeks of the college term and she to hers? But the young woman she was back then hadn't been comfortable with pushing, listening to her gut, acting from a position of confidence.

Over the years, the grief had faded from a terrible stabbing agony to something softer, and she found herself able to enjoy memories of Kyle as often as she considered his untimely death.

Beau broke into her reverie, helping her over an unsteady pile of gravel. "Mom still counts on Pioneer Day. It brings in enough to carry us for a month or two, and by then the summer contracts start rolling in. Also…"

"Also it means the world to her to participate, and she would be crushed if that didn't happen," she finished gently. "Your parents started the celebration, didn't they?"

He nodded. "Yeah. Mom mostly, but Dad talked the town council into it." Beau exhaled and his shoulders sagged. "Even the year Dad passed, Mom would not hear of bowing out."

Kara had kept hold of his hand and she squeezed his fingers. "Pioneer Day is still two days away. Tons can happen by then."

Like finding out his mother hadn't survived? Her mind buzzed. Not all searches ended happily. Sometimes at night she couldn't sleep, thinking of the people she hadn't saved, especially the six-year-old boy who'd wandered from his family camp and drowned in a pond a half mile from the tent where his family slumbered in oblivion. Millie and Phil had covered the half mile in a flash, but not soon enough to save him. She wouldn't ever forget that little still form, his blond hair floating around him like a halo.

"We're close to the top. Maybe…" Again, he didn't finish.

*Maybe we'll be able to spot Ree.*

He began to move faster, almost reaching a slow jog, until they hit the steepest section of trail. Beau was an athlete, he'd explained his fitness regimen at length to her, but even his six-mile runs and endless mountain biking adventures couldn't keep him from breathing hard. Kara was doing her share of panting.

The task was not simply climbing but trying to maintain their footing on ground slippery with wet leaves and loose gravel. As it was, she clutched his hand and went down onto her knee before he caught her.

They were both huffing when they reached the top, scrambling up onto the truck-sized slab of rain-polished granite. The view hitched her breath, God's grandeur spread out below them like a priceless tapestry. Meager pockets of lingering snow, reflecting the last rays of daylight, covered severe granite peaks that flowed into a wooded valley where she could make out the hatchery buildings in the distance.

Kara hugged herself. "Exquisite. I can see why she wants to make this accessible."

"It's been a dream of hers since she and Dad bought the property."

She felt a pang. *Then why did your mom ask me to sell it for her?* And why had she made Kara promise not to tell anyone? He had plenty of other things to worry about. He pulled out the binoculars and she did the same.

Mount Shasta poked up through a blanket of clouds, her top a crown of fleece. The foothills too held frosty coverings, and the cold made her fingers go numb around the lenses. A sharper focus allowed her to zoom in closer.

Below their granite perch, she picked out the lower trail that would provide a gentler but less convenient journey to the overlook. It appeared much longer than the direct route. The way would require traversing a giant log at one point that spanned a creek that was almost inundated by the spring snowmelt. That would prove a complication to her blind dog, but not enough to stop them.

"The stream's already looking pretty full," she said. "But I think we can get the dogs across unless the water level surges." It might require some finagling since Phil was not keen about water.

"Yes. This season's going to be a bear for flooding."

The snow had arrived early and stayed with relentless persistence. The ground already struggled to absorb the melt caused by a handful of sunny days.

"Mom wanted to start clearing it last month, but the snow didn't cooperate."

Kara had heard as much from Ree, though the woman hadn't gone into details.

They both scanned again for any minute indication of what had happened to her. It would be a long journey to get both dogs up the winding trail, over the granite perch and around to the site where they'd first detected. If Ree had been caught in the slide, the dogs could come close, but they'd need heavy equipment and outside resources to uncover her. Kara looked across the horizon, training her binoculars on the ridge of rock that had collapsed upon the trail where they'd been searching. Was his mom in there somewhere? Buried? Frightened and in pain?

Beau abruptly stowed his binoculars and turned to Kara, his expression resolute. "It's getting late. It's going to be a brutal, cold night. Radio your brother to come walk you down. Please."

"Beau, you know perfectly well it's too dangerous to stay out alone." She paused. "Your mother wouldn't want you to do this."

"And she wouldn't want you up here with me either."

She tried again. "One wrong step, and there would be nobody close to radio for help."

"Mom has no one, Kara." He gestured to the wild sprawl around them.

"Beau…"

He turned, bending slightly to gather her gaze in his. His intensity made her heart hammer. He reached out and touched her shoulders.

"My unit…" He breathed out and shook his head. "They wouldn't ever leave me or anyone else behind. Ever. That principle is drilled into every Marine from jump. How can I walk away from my own mother?"

She reached a finger up to stroke his cheek, as if she could draw some of the terrible pain out, the tarry fear.

"If we knew where she was, it would be different, but we can't trade one life for another."

"Not your life."

"Or yours either." Kara's radio crackled and she cleared her throat and answered.

"Sheriff Franco has made it to the rockfall area," her mother said. "He's examining the scene. He's got a team taking photos before it's completely dark." She paused. "As soon as he's done, he's going to hike up to meet you with Chase.

Garrett will follow when he arrives." The unsaid was clear: ...*since you refuse to come down.*

"Copy," Kara said. There was no use trying to prevent them all from coming. Her brothers would make the climb in spite of any argument from her. They'd bring blankets and more gear, maybe something warm to drink. That was a welcome thought since her limbs were numb with cold. It would still be a long, dangerous night for everyone.

Beau muttered to himself and looked once more at the fading sky before something inside him seemed to give. He gestured to her.

"One minute, Mom." When Kara lowered the radio, Beau cleared his throat.

"Tell them to hold in place. We'll come down."

His pain flowed into her at his agonizing decision. "Are you sure?"

She hadn't wanted to be the one to say it, but there had been no sign of his mother, and the treacherous terrain was being swallowed up by the coming gloom. Still, she wanted it to be his decision, since every hour increased the risk to his missing mother. He would be the one to live with the consequences of the decision.

"Are you really certain, Beau?"

"No, but I can't make the choice for everyone else. It's going to be dark in under two hours. Your brothers are coming up here, and the cops and everyone are going to risk their safety if I stay. I can't let that happen." His voice rang with anguish. "I can't ask them to do that. Or you." He took her hand. "Especially you."

She wanted to make it better somehow, reassure him that his choice was for the best, but she could offer no optimistic scenario. The fact was they had to keep themselves safe to continue the search the following day, and that meant leaving his mother to possibly face another night lost and exposed. It was a torturous truth of search and rescue. Searchers had to avoid becoming victims themselves.

She swallowed hard and thumbed the radio. "Hold all personnel, Mom. We're coming down now. We've identified a route for the morning."

"Affirmative," her mother said, her tone filled with relief. "Garret's brought the RV. We'll camp here tonight and muster at four a.m."

Kara clicked off and squeezed Beau's hand. He bent and rested his forehead on their joined hands.

"I know this is extremely difficult for you, Beau." She wanted desperately to comfort him, but he straightened, mouth twisted, and let go.

"We should climb down." But instead he stood there, immobile.

Why wouldn't he let her in? Was it his condition? His extreme duress? The memory of Kyle standing between them? He didn't know what she'd learned through Kyle's illness. God made people to stand together in their pain. Sometimes it was the only way to stand at all.

The frigid wind tore at their jackets, penetrating their clothing, causing their eyes to tear. She tugged his sleeve and they clambered down from their rock perch to a spot more protected, where they stood shivering, Beau lost in silent thought.

"Tell me what's going through your mind," she said, when she could no longer stand it. They could at least share that, couldn't they?

At first it seemed he would refuse. "I can't stop thinking about her lying out here somewhere for another night in the cold." He did turn to her then, eyes roving her face. "What if she's in pain? Bleeding?"

There was only one comfort she could share with him. "Let's pray." She knew he'd been raised a believer, just as she had. Was he still strong in his faith? Before she could second-guess herself, she reached out and wrapped her arms around him. His jacket was spangled with ice flecks, and she spoke quietly. She sent a plea to God that Ree would be protected, that tomorrow would bring a happy closure to the situation, that she would be restored to her friends and the son who loved her dearly.

His amen was strong and steady.

"Tomorrow we'll find her. I know we will," she whispered in his ear.

He didn't speak and she hugged him closer, wishing she could feel the steady beat of his heart. His arms around her were strong, rocking her gently from side to side as if he were the one offering comfort. It was so easy to let the embrace linger, to pretend they were the closest of friends like they'd been long before life got complicated, in the sunny summers spent exploring. He pressed his cheek atop her head and let out the deepest of sighs before he eased away, reinserting the distance between them.

They stood in silence side by side, waiting.

She squeezed her eyes shut and said another silent prayer for Beau.

Tonight would be one of the hardest of his life, and tomorrow might be even worse.

She only hoped the enemy out there was done interfering.

Beau made sure Kara stayed close as they moved to meet her brother, sharing as much warmth as they could. They were both shivering as they reached the slide area where some police officers were still working with the help of high-powered flashlights.

"Chase," Kara called out as her brother appeared, his tall form detaching from the shadows. He greeted them with a terse nod, still obviously upset but keeping his temper in check.

"Mom finally got in contact with the two other employees, Sonia and John. They weren't camping far from here, turns out, but they didn't get a signal until about an hour ago when they were driving back to the hatchery. They're here now. Sheriff's talking to them."

Which Beau took to mean no one had anything to add about his mom's possible whereabouts. He tried to absorb the disappointment. It was a fantasy to think Sonia and John would have revealed she was simply away somewhere.

No. Millie sensed his mom had recently been in the vicinity of the lower trail.

Beau nodded to the two officers in heavy jackets who were starting to pack up their gear. One held a plastic bag containing the blasted remnants of a stick of dynamite.

Excellent. Now there was at least some solid evidence they'd been attacked. It couldn't be chalked up to Beau's imagination or some random natural event. The officers were at the end of their shifts. They wouldn't be searching through the night for his mother either. Mechanically, he reached to help Kara over a sharp spine of rock at the same time Chase did.

He should withdraw and let her brother assist, but he didn't, placing an arm around her and guiding her. Chase's look was indecipherable. Annoyed? Surprised? Calculating? Beau suddenly didn't care. Maybe it was because he knew his best friend would want him to or because he and Kara had narrowly escaped death or just for the comfort it gave him to feel her close, but he led her to more secure footing and he didn't care about Chase's views on his behavior.

They'd come to the last turn before the hatchery when low rumbling caught Beau's ear.

"Garrett's hooking up the RV," Chase said. "We figured you wouldn't mind. Room for us and the dogs so we don't clutter up your floor."

He'd have been perfectly content with Kara's family taking up every square inch of the office building, but he knew they wouldn't be comfortable. Still, how comfy was it going to be for four people and as many dogs crammed into one trailer?

"You can take my room," he said to Kara. "I'll sleep in Mom's."

She shook her head. "No need. The RV fits six comfortably and the dogs all pile up anyway."

He didn't argue. He was too busy tutoring himself about who he was about to encounter— Franco, uniformed likely, and Kara's mom, an older, taller version of Kara with the same quick smile.

Sheriff Franco met them in the office, as expected in uniform with a helpful name tag. If only everyone wore name tags. Franco and Beth had a map spread out between them.

Beth embraced her daughter and nodded to Beau. "Glad to see you all back here in one piece. Coffee's brewed." She provided them both with steaming mugs.

Beau willed his hands not to shake as he gripped it.

Kara stopped to check on Phil and Millie, who were lying together in the tiny kitchen space. "Hey, babies. Happy to see me?"

Millie wagged her tail and licked Kara. Phil gave Kara a friendly poke with his nose.

A neatly dressed man who had to be a Wolfe joined them and clapped him on the shoulder. Dark hair, easygoing smile. "Haven't seen you in a dog's age, Beau, since I got cut from the water polo team and you didn't." He pointed to the droopy bloodhound at his ankle. "This here's Pinkerton, but his friends call him Pinky."

Beau smiled tightly. The clan must have been alerted to his prosopagnosia because they were lobbing clues like softballs. While he should no doubt appreciate it, he felt only mortification. Teeth gritted, he memorized every detail of Garrett's face, his relaxed posture, the color pattern on his drooling dog. "Good to see you too."

"Hey, Garrett," Kara said. "Is Catherine home?"

"She's with her uncle Orson, staying until his CT scan is done, but she sends her love and a request for your weeds and seeds muffin recipe."

Kara rolled her eyes and explained. "Chase calls them that just because I'm a vegetarian."

"Among your other cool attributes," Garrett said.

Beth beckoned them to the table. "Show us what you were thinking, Kara."

Kara traced it on the map. "We skirt the slide to the overlook. From there we can follow a trail to the lower pasture where Millie was signaling before. Hopefully she can pick up the scent again."

"We'll provide personnel to assist." Franco eased back in his chair. "We've gotten statements from all the employees and the neighbor. Nothing really helpful, no indication there had been any threats to your mother." His gunmetal gaze locked on Beau. "When you were here last, there was the...incident you reported."

"Incident"...that was better than "accident." Maybe Franco was starting to believe him.

"The incident," he went on, "and the hit-and-run Kara phoned about involving your truck. And now this paintball intruder and the slide."

Beau waited to hear the rest, the real point Franco was trying to make.

"Why does trouble follow when you come to town, Beau?"

The coffee burned his tongue.

"I don't know," he said slowly. "And I can't even think about that right now."

The sheriff's concerned expression spoke volumes. "Understood. But I'm beginning to wonder if all these misfortunes might stem from what happened that night."

"That night that you didn't believe me?" Frustration broke through his self-control. "You thought I'd imagined it? Maybe been drinking?"

Franco didn't back away from Beau's anger. "There was no evidence to indicate a crime had occurred."

"Plenty of evidence that something's wrong now though, huh?"

"If it's connected, we'll find that out."

Beau plunked down his mug, sloshing coffee. "With all due respect, Sheriff, I don't care what is connected to what right now. Mom is all that matters."

"Agreed. I'll dig into the other possibilities, but locating your mother is the top priority for all of us."

He nodded, anger still simmering. True, finding his mother was top of the list. But he would not stop there. Sheriff Franco could keep up his investigations, but Beau would be digging right along too.

Because someone had targeted his mother and nearly killed him and Kara today.

And that someone was going to answer for what they'd done.

# SIX

Kara fumbled her way into consciousness hours later, groggy, sluggish as she climbed from her lower bunk in the RV, pulled on clothes and washed her face. Chase's rattling snores from the far end of the trailer indicated he had no such problems sleeping. In the kitchenette, she filled bowls for Millie and Phil and set them to munching.

Tank and Pinkerton were already similarly occupied, slopping kibble and water across the floor. A glance out the window revealed a fat slice of moon gleaming off the hatchery buildings. Lights in the office shone both upstairs and downstairs. She wondered if Beau had gotten any sleep at all. She had only experienced short bursts that hadn't been enough to replenish her energy.

Her brother Garrett was his usual cheerful self as he turned off the tiny stove. More cheerful than he'd ever been before he'd met Catherine.

Most of her family had paired off, it seemed. She felt the tiniest stab of envy about her sister Steph's upcoming wedding to be held at their Security Hounds Ranch. Steph and Vance were a textbook case of opposites attracting: the serious, efficient Steph and her playful, fun-loving Vance. So were her brother Garrett and his fiancée. Not to mention her brother Roman and his wife. Kara and Chase were the only singles of the bunch now, unless one counted her widowed mother. So many happy partnerships. She thought of the wedding dress in her own closet, never worn, since Kyle had died before the ceremony. There would always be an ache when she remembered him, but the pain was survivable after four years. Kyle was a quiet, cerebral person, not as gregarious as his best friend, Beau O'Connor.

"Cops aren't here yet." Garrett offered her egg and cheese sandwiched in an English muffin. There were four more, wrapped in foil, smelling of bacon.

"Thanks, Gare." She took a bite, though her stomach was already tense and her appetite nonexistent. Nourishment before an arduous search was mandatory. It was going to be a very long day. "How's Catherine?" She knew he'd called her the night before.

That lovely sheen of happiness overlaid his expression. "She's keeping her head above water."

Doing better than that, Kara suspected. Catherine was as strong as they came, nursing her sick uncle and trying to hold the threads of her broken family together. She was tough, kind and intelligent, a suitable match for Kara's darling brother. On impulse, she kissed him on the cheek. "I'm glad. Catherine and I are going to take that vegetarian cooking class, you know."

He pressed a hand to his stomach. "Remind me to stock the fridge with meaty foods before you do."

She laughed. "You're going to learn to love eggplant, someday." She nibbled at her sandwich as she peered through the blinds. "Who's out there talking to mom? The two with the horses?"

"Neighbor, I think, and a hatchery worker. They wanted to help with the search."

Chase's snore reverberated through the trailer. They'd all learned to bring ear plugs when they shared sleeping space.

"Big surprise, Sleeping Beauty hit the Snooze button. He'll be ready for the kickoff. Grumpy but conscious." Garrett lowered his head to catch her eye. "And how about you, little sis? You up for this today?"

She rubbed one socked foot over the other and

forced herself to eat another bite. "Sure. I didn't get hurt in the slide yesterday."

"Not talking about the slide, as you fully well know. How's it going being around Beau?"

Garrett knew. He always read the emotions rippling underneath. She didn't have to spell it out for him, how Beau had hurt her, stepping out of their friendship when she got engaged, how she'd never understood why Kyle's best friend danced uneasily at the fringes of his lingering illness instead of jumping in with both feet. How the last straw had snapped when Beau had left the hospital and their fragile, rebuilt relationship behind.

When she didn't answer, he poked her toes playfully with his boot. "What's the name of his memory problem again?"

Tactful way to put it. "Face blindness. That's a heavy weight on him."

Garrett was silent a moment. "That's right. On him, not you. Don't do that thing where you take on someone else's suffering until it crushes you, huh?"

Because she'd already done that with Kyle, and it had almost defeated her. Only God saved her from being extinguished under the weight, God and the Wolfe family He'd blessed her with. Loving and failing to save Kyle had cut a piece of her heart away, but it had strengthened her belief in herself. She knew she could survive the worst because she'd already done it.

At least with Beau, there was no love involved. Garrett was still gazing at her.

"We're here to find his mother. That's all."

"Mm-hmm." Garrett drank his coffee.

She finished the sandwich, tied on her boots and grabbed her pack. The dogs were already standing as she threw her napkin away. Garrett's bloodhound, Pinkerton, was the epitome of easygoing. He wagged his tail in anticipation. Her own emotions were laced with dread as she strapped Security Hounds vests on all the dogs except Phil and leashed Millie. Phil attached himself to Millie's side, butting the good natured Pinkerton out of the way.

They exited the trailer, their breath immediately puffing white in the frigid spring morning. Her mom hastened over.

"Garrett and Chase are assigned to the outlook, where they can launch a drone. They'll be close if you need any backup. Franco will accompany you and the dogs."

Kara hoped the officer was in good shape. The trail was long, and from what they'd seen the previous day, it looked like a killer. She frowned. Bad choice of words. "Where's Beau?"

"Haven't seen him yet."

She was processing this surprise when Beth

led them to the others and made the formal introductions between the Wolfe family and Ree's staff.

"This is Natalie Clark," she said, gesturing. Natalie's curly hair was pulled into a loose bunch on the back of her neck. In the dim light, the woman, probably in her early sixties, looked the same as Kara remembered, athletic with an air of energy. "She owns the stables adjacent. And this is John Partridge. He and his wife, Sonia, work for Ree."

Natalie held the reins of a sturdy mare and John did the same with a horse so dark it almost blended in with the predawn gloom.

"I thought we could help. Cover the Mesquite Trail since that one's hard to hike on foot. It joins up with the Overlook Trail past the river. Ree didn't borrow a horse, so it'd be unlikely she went that way, but we have to be thorough, right?" Natalie's horse draped his head over her shoulder and lipped her hair. She stroked the velvet muzzle.

John didn't appear as easy around his horse. His goatee was flecked with silver that caught the porch lights.

His wife, Sonia, exited the small cabin and joined the group, offering the horse the core of the apple she'd just finished. She cocked her head at her husband and folded her arms, accentuating her wide shoulders. "Is this a good idea? A horseback trek before dawn? You're not the most skilled cowboy, John."

"We have to find Ree soon or..." He shrugged.

Kara's stomach tightened another notch. John was right. Soon... Ree's survival window was running out.

"Okay. Be careful. I'll help search on foot if someone will tell me where."

Beth discussed a plan with Sonia that would both keep her safe and out of the way of the dog search teams.

Kara scanned for Beau. Where was he? Had he broken his word and gone searching for his mother on his own the previous night? Thoughts about all the dangers he might have encountered made her skin prickle.

Sheriff Franco pulled up in his car just as Beau appeared from the trees on the graveled path. She breathed a sigh of relief. Beau slowed his steps. Sizing up the group, she realized, trying to remember if they were people he knew.

She felt a pang.

Even after their intense hours of struggle the previous day and decades of friendship, she might be a total stranger to Beau O'Connor this morning. She had to do something to help.

"Sheriff Franco," she said loudly. "You know my brother Garrett. And you've met Ree's staff?"

She quickly rattled off their names. "Chase will join us in a minute."

Franco nodded. "Yes, Miss Wolfe. I've met everyone."

Beau was dressed in jeans and a warm jacket, a pack slung over his shoulder. His gaze caught her first. "Morning. I climbed the fire tower. No helpful intel, but at least it kept me busy. Ground's muddy and there's still some snow, maybe patches of ice. Weather looks to be cold and clear."

She drew alongside and bumped his shoulder with hers. "Thanks for the report. Ready to tackle the trail?"

His gaze roved her face, her hair, down her arms to her hands, memorizing or recognizing, she wasn't sure, but the warmth in his tone reassured her that he knew her. "Ready, Kara."

"Me too."

The door to the smaller residence slammed open, and Vince stalked out, haggard, wearing the same clothes he'd been in the day before.

"Vince," Sheriff Franco said. "You helping with the search?"

"Not until later. We got two trout pickups this morning, first thing." He fired a look at Beau. "Unless you're gonna take care of that?"

"I'm looking for Mom." *End of story*, Beau's tone said. "Deliveries can wait."

"Yeah, well your mom isn't gonna want to eat the cost of two orders, nor take the flack for not meeting the terms of the contracts."

"They'll understand," Beau said low and even.

"But your mom won't and you know it." He waved a dismissive hand. "Never mind. I'll deal with it. Looks like there are plenty of searchers already."

"Where's Chase?"

Beth's question was answered as Chase slogged from the trailer, jacket flapping open and boots untied. He accepted the coffee from his mother, slugged half of it down and winced.

"Did you miss the memo with the departure time?" Garrett teased.

"I'm here, aren't I? Twenty seconds early, so quit your bellyaching."

"See what I meant about grumpy?" Garrett stage-whispered.

Franco double-checked that everyone would be funneling information to Beth, who was connected via radio to him. "No dangerous risk-taking. I've briefed you all about the attacks."

"Like the paintball guy?" Natalie said.

"If you see anyone who doesn't belong, radio immediately. Right now we have one possible victim. Let's keep it that way."

One victim. Kara suppressed a shiver.

John and Natalie mounted the horses and rode toward the tree line.

Chase retrieved the bulky drone case from the van while Garrett followed with the two dogs. Franco lagged behind.

"Are you okay, Sheriff?" Kara asked.

He waved her off. "Fine, fine. Sciatica slows me down. I'll bring up the rear."

She and Beau surged ahead behind Millie and Phil. Millie's giant ears streamed out like sails as she trotted in tandem with her counterpart. Millie had quickly learned that trusting in Phil's proximity generally enabled her to ramble the world without stumbling. He was a stalwart companion who knew her every move. Like Kyle had been to Kara. For years thoughts of Kyle would be accompanied by excruciating pain. Now the memories also held a portion of joy. That thought made her smile as they hustled along for the first half mile.

A squirrel chittered at them as they reached the slide and began their detour. Millie turned her head to the scolding and gulped in big nosefuls of air while Phil scared the rodent away with one deep-throated woof. If only their other problems could be solved so easily.

There was no space for small talk. Garrett and Chase with their dogs set a brisk pace. Franco had begun to fall far behind her and Beau. The mood wasn't right either. Every mile they covered ratcheted the tension higher until her nerves felt like overstretched wire. She couldn't wait to get Millie on the scent again, confident the dog would lead them right to Beau's mother.

*Hang on, Ree. Please.*

With only one stop for water and snacks, Millie and Phil were still brimming with energy, and they reached the overlook much faster than they'd done the night before. At the base of the granite perch, Chase stopped and looked as though he was going to tell them to delay until he got the drone launched, but she was already breathless with their eager pace.

"Where's the sheriff?" he demanded.

Franco was a good quarter mile behind.

"He'll catch up." She hadn't offered the scent article to Millie yet because the dog would be continually wanting to circle back to the rubble. Before her brothers could protest, she moved toward the giant cap of rock. Without her asking, Beau hoisted Millie and started to climb. She and Phil scrambled behind. Garrett and Chase shouldered their gear and prepared to do the same.

The sun was just beginning to bronze the sky when they made it to the top. Beau put Millie down and Kara kept a close hold on her leash while they pulled out binoculars, no noise but the wind and the voices of her brothers as they prepped the drone.

No sign of an intruder, nor any hint that would lead them to Ree.

Without a word, she and Beau continued on. They spent the five minutes picking their way down from the giant rock, which fortunately had broken into steplike fragments on one side. Franco's sciatica would likely be an issue, but with Beau carrying Millie, they made it down quickly.

"Drone up," Chase reported via the radio. "I'll have eyes for you imminently."

"Copy." When her cell phone beeped, she opened the drone app. Beau pushed close, his cheek almost to hers. It felt strange, being this near someone who wasn't Kyle, but comforting too. Beau wasn't an intimate friend anymore, but her heart didn't seem to know that. He smelled of clean soap and the woods, a heady combination.

"No sign of any bad guys," Chase said.

"But no sign of my mother either?"

"Negative. We'll move the zone off trail, more southward."

"Copy," Kara said. She commanded the dogs to get their focus and brought out the plastic bag with the seed scoop. "Millie's going on scent now."

She took a firm hold on Millie's leash. "All right, baby. Here we go. Find."

\* \* \*

Beau savored the warmth of being close to Kara. He shook off the sensation and stuck by her. It was an effort. After an enormous whiff from the bag containing Ree's birdseed scoop, Millie practically hurtled downslope. Phil kept pace at her side, diverting them around branches and dips in the rutted ground. He was elated. Millie had managed to pick up his mother's scent again from this side of the slide. Why had she come this way? Where had she gone?

Beau heard the rippling water as they continued their frantic flight down the valley. The ground was spongy and clung to his boots. The dogs squelched along without hesitation as they covered a quarter mile, then a half, moving steadily toward the river. It made no sense to him, but if the dogs decided it was the right way, he'd trust them, and their handler too.

Kara leapt and sprinted as she kept close to her charges.

Several miles past the log bridge was the Mesquite Trail, where John and Natalie would be searching. Between them, they'd undoubtedly find her. The horses would enable Natalie and John to assist with a transport unless the ground was too saturated.

In that case, Beau would carry his mom out. His pulse roared almost out of control.

Millie stopped so fast that Phil barely had a moment to react. Beau skidded on the wet ground, trying to grab for Kara. He looked around the grassy foothills. "I don't see anything. Has she got something?"

Kara looked puzzled, as if she hadn't expected Millie's sudden detour either. Phil stuck with Millie, hip-checking her out of the way of several rocks poking up. "We'll give her a few minutes, and if we're going in circles I'll refresh the scent with her."

*Don't fail me now, Millie.*

The dog suddenly zoomed through the tall grass and pockets of snow. Incredible, considering she was being guided purely by smell. She paralleled the trail for twenty yards and then abruptly stopped again, shaking her massive propeller ears.

"What's wrong? Has she lost the scent?"

"I don't think so. More likely she got more than one trail to follow." Kara offered her another sniff of the birdseed scoop. Millie remained still for one moment, head cocked as if she was thinking, and then she took off back toward the trail, and soon they were jogging in the direction of the log bridge again. Beau had a feeling deep down that they'd been getting close.

It was all Kara could do to keep up with Millie's progress as she steamed toward the bridge,

Phil galloping along. The river loomed perilously close.

When Kara gave the halt command, Millie ignored her, yanking the leash, coming closer and closer to the thundering water. With a sudden break, she pulled the leash from Kara's grip.

"Halt, Millie!" Kara shouted. Beau lunged to grab Millie, but Phil solved the problem his own way. He leapt atop Millie's wide shoulders and brought her to the ground.

Millie whined in complaint, but Phil pinned her until Kara could snatch the leash again.

"Good job, Phil," she panted as she soothed the bloodhound. Phil rolled off his companion but stuck close.

Beau jogged past them to the log bridge, scanning the swirling water. The banks were brushy and overgrown, the branches piled high enough to partially obscure the view on both sides.

Millie howled her displeasure at being stopped.

"She wants to cross," Kara said slowly. "And she's reacting like she's close to her target."

Her target. His mother.

Beau nodded. "I should cross alone, but there's miles of scrub here. It would take me hours to search without Millie's help." Beyond the bridge, the path meandered away, overgrown and uneven. Even more distance to cover.

Kara echoed his own thoughts. "Do you think your mom would have come this way?"

"Honestly, I can't think of one reason why she would have. This trail links up with Mesquite; that's the horse trail. She wouldn't have attempted it on foot. Even on horseback it's rough going." He looked at her. "You wait here with the dogs."

She shook her head. "Like you said, it will take hours to search without Millie's nose."

Her phone buzzed. "A text from Franco. 'Unable to join. Holding in place here.'"

"So much for police backup."

She responded, then called her brothers on speaker. "Can you focus the drone along the riverbank by the log bridge?"

Chase replied, "That's a negative for the moment. We've got a malfunction, so we need to change out the batteries."

She stood, and Phil eased off Millie, ready to leap on her again if necessary. Beau saw Kara roll her shoulders as if she were coming to a decision that he wasn't going to like. "I'll cross with Millie. You can follow with Phil if he'll do it. He's not a big water dog."

"No," Beau started but she cut him off.

"I need to take Millie. I'm her handler and she trusts me. The log's plenty wide enough to accommodate us. It's been in place for decades, you said."

"Yes," he admitted. "I've crossed it plenty of times, but…"

"Then I shouldn't have any trouble."

He fisted his hands on his hips. "Carrying a hundred-pound dog?"

"Ninety." Kara stared him down, and again he noted how her strength had changed in profound, immeasurable ways. He felt a flicker of pride in her, along with a surge of worry.

"I can do this," she said. "I wouldn't risk my dog if I couldn't."

"We should hike downstream where it's shallower. The water's high, freezing. If you slip…"

"Your mom's here, Beau. Close. Millie knows it."

Her certainty pinned him in place. But if Kara fell…

Millie whined.

She bent down and gave Millie the command. In a moment, the big dog jumped onto her back, paws over her shoulders. It took all Kara's quad strength and Beau's helping hand to get her to her feet with Millie's weight on her back, but she did it. He marveled.

Phil growled, shaking himself.

"Phil is not a fan of this idea." Kara resettled Millie across her shoulders.

Beau grimaced. "Neither am I. I'd still rather you let me carry her across."

"Phil would have an issue with that. He hasn't learned to trust you yet."

And neither had she, likely. He was certainly different from the man she'd known, the third musketeer with her and Kyle. He'd not trusted her with his darkest moment. Why should she trust him now?

She tucked her arms behind her back to support Millie's hind end, and the dog aided the process by leaning tight against her shoulders. Beau gripped her forearm, the best he could do for them.

"Okay, girl. Here we go," Kara said.

*Be careful. Go slow. Better yet, change your mind.* None of the thoughts made it past his clenched teeth. The log was almost ten inches wide, the remnants of what had been a gargantuan tree. The river water lapped the underside thanks to the snowmelt, a swirling ice-cold torrent. If they slipped, they'd be in for a frigid plunge and a swift journey downstream. He'd get them out, but it wouldn't be easy, and by then they could both be hypothermic. And if Kara hit her head when she tumbled…

Beau could sense the electricity still cascading through Millie's furry body. She was close to finding Ree and she knew it. Her nose would not be denied, even if it meant an awkward piggyback ride over a swollen river.

As predicted, Phil barked his displeasure. Kara gave him a firm "hold in place" command.

Beau felt united with Phil over their mutual discomfort.

"Two stubborn females." Phil's lip curled as if he agreed completely.

Beau fished the radio from his pocket as Chase's voice blared out loud and clear. No doubt he'd been scanning with binoculars while the drone was repaired.

"You are not going to do that, Kara," he snapped.

"I already tried to talk her out of it," Beau said.

"Let me do it then. There's no way…"

But she ignored her brother and stepped onto the log.

As soon as she put weight on the wood, it shifted.

How? The beam was firmly anchored by sturdy stones. He reached for her, but the log spun under her feet.

She was plunged headfirst, pulling out of his grasp, falling toward the swirling water.

# SEVEN

Kara's stomach flipped as she tumbled toward the water. Her palms hit the wood log, and she felt it roll. The log was now a shifting cylinder, detached from its foundations on one side and threatening to come free of the opposite bank in short order.

She grabbed for Millie and felt the dog sliding from her back.

Toes gripping the wet wood, she fought to steady herself. One foot plunged into water so cold it numbed her instantly.

It was no use, the free end of the trunk was being sucked away from the bank, along with her and Millie. It slowly rotated, and she knew they were seconds away from being thrown into the river.

As her fingers lost their grip, she felt something anchoring her in place. Beau had her by the sleeve. With a grunt, he hauled her onto the log where Millie was still precariously clinging by her front legs. Kara grasped one wet paw, and it was enough that Millie was able to slither fully onto the wood surface again.

"Cross to the other side," Beau urged and she scrambled, tugging Millie across the rolling log to the far bank, somersaulting with her into the brush. Feet sinking in the mud, she pulled herself up and out, with Millie at her side until they both made it to semi firm ground.

Millie lathered her face with a sloppy tongue. She hugged her, heart full. Her baby was safe, but *Beau…* He'd been right behind her, but he hadn't made it to the bank.

"Hold," she told the dog.

Heart pounding, she did a one-eighty and scrambled back to the river, searching. Beau was huddled on the log that was still barely attached at one end, the other bouncing violently on the waves. The whole thing would be pulled loose at any moment.

He was stomach down, shouting at something, and she pushed closer to see over the brambles.

"Phil," Beau called out. "Here, boy."

Her nerves turned to ice as she ascertained that Phil had dived straight in when he'd seen her and Millie struggling. He could swim—she'd seen him paddling across a pond with no trouble. She recalled in nauseating detail that he'd swum out with her to retrieve the little boy they'd been too late to rescue. Ever since that moment though, Phil had detested the water. She'd always believed it was because he too felt he'd failed, lost a little soul whom they should have saved.

Phil was paddling furiously, but his rounded eyes told her he was starting to panic as the water pulled him away from his people.

"Phil!" she screamed, but the torrent swallowed up her words.

Beau crawled the length of the precarious log, shoved the radio and his phone at Kara, and before she could rally one syllable, he turned and dove in, strong strokes defying the force as he fought. She could not breathe as she watched him struggling to close the gap. What if he drowned trying to save her dog? His fingers grazed Phil's head, but a swell yanked the animal away.

Kara bit her lip until she tasted blood. The water was too strong, too cold. Fear clawed at her insides. She grabbed the radio, but what good would it do? Her brothers were far away, the sheriff even farther. She mumbled panicked prayers.

*Please, God. Please.*

Head down, Beau cleaved the water as if it were an enemy, like he'd done all those years ago for water polo. Only now he was fully grown, his body and spirit toughened by the Marines. With a massive effort, he grabbed Phil's collar.

Beau tugged and kicked, attempting to tow them toward the log, but he could not make enough headway. *Help them, Kara. You're all they have.*

How? She could toss the rope she had coiled in her backpack, but it would take time to unpack it. Instead, she scooped up a stout branch and shoved it out toward them. "Grab it, Beau."

Had he heard her over the roar? She didn't think so at first, but he finally managed to grip the branch with one fist, clinging to Phil with the other. She leaned with all her might in the opposite direction. Her feet sank in the mud, and her arms quivered, but she held steady.

One sticky footstep at a time, she towed them toward the bank.

Beau hooked his elbow around the branch and kept hold of Phil with the other until she brought them close enough for him to reach the fringe of shrubbery. He clung there, panting, grabbing an armful of prickly foliage.

"I'm anchored," he said. "Can you get Phil?"

She let go of her rescue branch, slogged closer until she could barely grab one paw. Phil struggled to her, plowing through the brambles until at last he climbed out, panting and dripping. "Guide," she told him and he sloshed immediately to Millie and took his place at her side. Millie began to lavish him with kisses, whining her concern for her friend.

Kara returned her attention to Beau, but he was pulling his own way clear by using the branches as grips, until he dropped to his knees next to her.

She threw her arms around his shoulders and hugged him. "That was too close. Way too close," she managed.

"I concur," he said, gulping in breaths. "We gotta give Phil some lessons in acceptable risk-taking."

"And you too." She wiped the water from his face, heart pounding double time in her chest. She kissed his cheek. "Thank you for rescuing my dog."

He smiled. "Anything for you, Henny Penny."

With trembling hands she pressed the radio button, but her brothers were already alerted, having got the drone up.

"We're coming to you. Mom contacted the sheriff and John and Natalie. Do you need a helicopter assist?"

"Negative. We're wet but uninjured. Going to check the dogs now. Wait one."

She went to examine Phil who sat miserably next to Millie. She caressed his head. "Oh, sweetie boy. I know you were trying to help Millie, but you could have drowned."

Phil dropped his head as if he were humiliated at having required a rescue. She dried them both off with towels she'd had bagged in her pack. Millie sat and endured it, but not patiently. Her body was tense under Kara's palms.

Tense because of what they'd experienced? No.

Kara turned to Beau, who was standing, shivering, water streaming from his wet clothing, his attention riveted to the bank. He looked from the water to Millie and finally up to her.

"Help will be here soon." He paused, a question in his eyes.

She nodded. "Millie wants to finish the search. We're close now."

"Are the dogs up to it? Are you?" Even in his desperation, he was giving her an out.

She stood, legs trembling only a little. After such a shock, she normally would hustle both dogs to shelter, to warmth and recovery.

But Millie was telling her in every sniff, whine and shuffle that the end was near.

Very near.

Kara's mouth went dry, and she did not allow herself to consider what that might mean.

Slowly she stood, and Millie and Phil leapt to their feet.

"Find," she said.

And she prayed.

\* \* \*

Beau knew there was something wrong in the way the log had failed, but he couldn't divert attention to the matter. With each yard of mucky ground they covered, his nerves ratcheted tighter.

Millie bayed, the mournful sound cutting through the weak sunshine. Phil raced shoulder to shoulder with his companion until Millie barreled up to a dense cluster of tall grass and stopped dead, emitting another eerie yowl.

Beau shoved the foliage out of the way.

A woman lay curled on her side, clothes muddy, face stark white, eyes closed. He dropped to his knees, vaguely aware of Kara congratulating the dogs and giving them rewards.

The cropped hair and the hoop earrings…

This was his mother.

"Mom," he rasped, fingers shaking as he sought for a pulse. He felt nothing. He tried again as Kara talked into the radio. The drone zoomed above them.

She couldn't be dead. Not this person who had been by his side through everything, the death of his dad, enlisting in the Marines, losing Kyle, the prosopagnosia. He'd never told her how he felt about Kyle and Kara, but he suspected she knew anyway. She was like that. He bent and pressed his face to hers because his skin knew, deep down in his cells, what the piece of his brain did not. She would always be a part of him.

"Mom..." he whispered.

A tiny puff of air, the merest tickle of her breath lit him from the inside out.

"She's breathing."

Kara was already handing him emergency blankets, which he used to ease between his mom and the cold ground as he did a cursory examination. No broken bones that he could see, no obvious bleeding except from a cut on her cheekbone, muddy and crusted over. But she was cold, so cold. He covered her with another blanket and gently chafed her arm.

"Mom, can you hear me?"

He felt Kara's hand on his bicep as he stroked his mother's hair, praying she would be able to feel him there with her.

"The sheriff says he can land a chopper in fifteen minutes if we can move her away from the river," Kara said. "John and Natalie are here."

He tried to formulate a plan as the two guided their horses over.

"You found her." Natalie slid off her horse. "Is she...?" Her eyes were huge under the puff of bangs.

"Alive," he said. "Chopper's en route, but we have to get her to a drier spot."

John hurried over. "What should I do?"

Chase spoke over the radio, pinpointing a location east that appeared more solid.

The sheriff's voice was next. "ETA twelve minutes for the chopper."

"We can carry her on the blanket." Beau organized the rescuers.

The four of them each took a corner and lifted. His mother didn't react, didn't stir. Trying not to let that worry him, he focused on keeping the movement as smooth as possible.

After what seemed like hours, the chopper appeared, and medics loaded his mother aboard. By the time the aircraft was whirling away, he could see Kara's brothers at the other side of the log.

"Why don't they cross?" John blinked. "What happened to the bridge?"

"It came loose when we climbed on it."

Natalie looked closer at Beau. "Is that why you're sopping wet?"

He nodded. "I've got to get to the hospital."

"Well, you're not getting back that way," John said, jerking a thumb where the bridge used to be.

Natalie frowned. "I'll go ride back and bring two more horses." She glanced at Millie and Phil.

John shook his head. "That will take a good hour or more."

Natalie exhaled. "What's the faster alternative?"

Engine noise snagged their attention. An ATV sped at them from the direction of the horse trail. Beau's heart leapt as a man got out.

"Vince?" Kara said, quieting Phil.

"Where is she? What's happened? Saw the helicopter."

"She's alive," Beau said. "Can you get us back to my truck? Bridge is out."

"Sonia told me. I called a buddy of mine in town and he brought his ATV. I can get you two and the dogs around the overlook and to the office in twenty minutes. Let's go."

How did Sonia know about the log bridge? But the question didn't slow him down as he gathered the gear. Kara loaded the dogs in the ATV.

"We'll ride back. Meet you at the hospital," Natalie said, but he hardly heard. His mind was galloping ahead, praying they hadn't been too late.

*Sheriff Franco, Chase, Garrett.* He reminded himself of the players as they bumped close to the log bridge. The sheriff was taking photos. He was standing, favoring one leg as if the climb down the overlook had taken its toll.

He held up a hand and Vince reluctantly stopped, grumbling as much as Beau was. Everything in him craved to be in motion, moving closer toward his mother, but they got out. Chase was on his hands and knees, staring at the spot where the log had come loose.

Vince spoke out the window. "On our way back. What's the problem?"

The sheriff leaned toward the window. "Need to talk to you two." He pointed to Kara and Beau. "Get your statement about what happened."

"No problem, but not now," Beau said.

"While it's fresh."

"You can meet us at the hospital." There was no way he was going to delay getting to his mother.

"The log didn't come loose by itself," Chase interjected.

Kara jerked a look at her brother. "What?"

"It was dug out on one end, the stabilizing stones were removed," Garrett confirmed.

Part of him was not surprised. Sabotage. And he'd allowed Kara and Millie to take the risk. His skin crawled.

"Someone didn't want you or anyone else to get across," Franco said.

*Why? They didn't want his mother found?*

"Kara, stay with your brothers," he started to say, but the expression on her face was half fury, half confusion and one hundred percent determined.

"Vince, get us back to the office, okay?" Kara said. "Beau needs to get to Ree, and my dogs should be rested and fully dried. I'll share what I know with you back there, Sheriff."

Vince didn't wait for confirmation. They piled in and he stomped the gas, flying over the rocky ground, heading up and around the overlook.

Beau gritted his teeth, willing the vehicle to move faster.

When they reached the office, he leapt out and ran for his keys, stopping only long enough to yank on dry clothes. He was still cold to the core, but Kara stopped him as he was about to bolt to his truck.

She gripped his hand. "I'll join you as soon as I can."

Her touch was the only thing that could have held him in place. "I'm sorry I got you involved in this...whatever it is."

"I'm not." She tipped her chin up. "You're my friend, Beau. And you were Kyle's too. I care about you and I'm going to help you through this."

Her eyes picked up the meager spring sunshine, and he wanted to jump into that soothing pool, the sparkling color that reminded him of the lush spring days of their youth. Though he knew he shouldn't, he clasped her to him, circling her tight. He couldn't make himself say a word, but he hoped she'd feel his gratitude and his deep affection that had never waned, even when she'd fallen in love with his best friend.

When he let her go, he saw the woman standing behind her who shared her smile. Kara's mother.

"Thank you," he managed. "And the team. For finding her."

"We'll pray, Beau."

And he was praying, too, as he sprinted for the door.

Phil shook himself as Beau moved by. The dog had been crushed that he hadn't been able to complete his mission to save Millie in the river. He could relate. How had he gone from a man who managed a platoon of four vehicles, sixteen soldiers and their multi-million-dollar equipment to someone who needed help to recognize his own mother? His childhood friend?

But Phil had jumped in that water, heedless of the risk of drowning.

Beau intended to keep jumping in too. Alone. He was grateful for the Security Hounds team, but he was relieved the search part was over.

Because whoever was trying to ruin his life would not get a chance to hurt Kara and her family. Of that, he was certain.

Now it was all on him.

# EIGHT

Kara and her mother completed a more thorough check of the dogs and found no injuries. Her brothers arrived as she was starting to text Garrett to arrange a ride to the hospital. She'd suggested a taxi first, but with the paintball attack fresh in her mind, she acquiesced to Garrett's strong suggestion that he drive her while Chase prepared the trailer for departure.

"Franco's on his way to the hospital so he'll likely get your statement there. We'll button things up here," Chase said. "Meet you back at home."

*Home.* Their work at the hatchery was finished in his mind. Normally when a search was completed, the Security Hounds team would depart quietly and leave the family to make their arrangements, a job well done. She didn't feel any sense of closure this time. She nodded absently. Millie snuffled in her direction and she went to her. "You were a star, little lady. With your nose

and Phil's eyes, there's no better partnership."
Millie leaned into her caress, and she gave her a
deep neck massage, which elicited a sigh of con-
tentment that puffed her fleshy lips. Phil quietly
observed their interaction, as relaxed as he was
capable of being.

"And you, Sergeant Phil, will be getting an
extra nice chew rope when we get home." Phil
had a thing for chew ropes. He didn't ever chew
them, but he adored adding new ones to the col-
lection he stored in his outdoor kennel.

Sonia let herself into the office, arms full, and
Garrett rushed to help her with the stack of boxes
she carried.

"Has there been an update?" she said.

"Ree is being transported to the hospital. That's
all we know."

"Wow. Incredible she's still alive." Sonia looked
at her curiously. "That was some rescue at the
river. Beau's a strong swimmer to drag that big
dog out."

"How did you know about that?" Kara asked.

Sonia lifted a shoulder. "I climbed the fire
watch tower to get a better look. Saw the whole
thing through my binoculars. Vince was finished
dealing with the deliveries when I climbed down,
so I told him. He said he'd borrow an ATV to
come up and help since the bridge was out." She
fingered her braid. "Weird, right? That log was

always so sturdy. I've been over it a dozen times since we moved here, and it never so much as wiggled."

It had sure done more than wiggle.

*The log didn't come loose by itself.*

"Why do you think Ree would be down there, Sonia?"

"At the river? I've no idea. Especially since her focus was sprucing up the trail. And that was kinda unusual in the first place. I haven't known her as long as Vince and Natalie, but I heard she'd been hemming and hawing over that trail improvement for years. Then all of a sudden it's full speed ahead? Wonder why she'd do that?" Sonia's gaze was pointed.

Was it a challenge Kara heard in her words? Did she know that Ree intended to list the property for sale? How would she? No one had been present during their meeting in Ree's tiny kitchen except the two of them. Kara remained silent until Sonia gestured to the supplies she'd brought in.

"Anyway, I don't know what I'm supposed to do with all this stuff now in light of the current situation."

"What is it?"

"Scavenger hunt maps and kid craft materials for Pioneer Day."

Kara sagged. The mega event had slipped completely from her thoughts. She eyed the colorful banner snapping in the breeze: *Welcome to the O'Connor Fish Hatchery.* The picnic tables looked as though they'd been washed, the small cement stage and amphitheater hosed clean where Ree, or maybe John, Sonia or Vince would give their talks about the life cycle of the fish they raised. Someone had already delivered folding chairs to supplement seating for the live music performances.

"Have to cancel, I guess," Sonia said. "Bummer. Should I call the chair of the event committee?"

"Not yet." Kara was surprised at her own statement. "Not without talking to Beau or Ree."

Sonia arched her brow. "But Beau's not..."

The owner? And he didn't even know that his mother was planning on selling the property. The hope she'd seen in his expression when he'd shared that he'd be moving back to Pine Bluff made her stomach clench. What would happen when he learned the truth that she'd been asked to keep from him? That the place where he'd chosen to restart his life would no longer belong to the O'Connor family?

Kara had been carefully preparing the listing and it had already gone out to a few brokers. She'd call and let them know everything was on hold, including the interested party who intended to show up for Pioneer Day to scope out the potential. It had felt so good to step into her role as a real estate agent, and the property would have established her in the area, but now she wished Ree hadn't approached her, at least not now. It was no longer simply a land transaction with Beau involved.

Kara dismissed the musings. No matter what the uncertainties, Ree depended on Pioneer Day financially. She kept her gaze firm. "Leave the things here. I'm on my way to see Beau and Ree right now."

Sonia's doubtful expression remained. "Okay. Guests have been calling for last-minute picnic reservations. Do I just keep adding them?"

Kara felt her brothers' eyes on her and she pushed back the uncertainty. "Of course. Things should go forward as planned. We can arrange for refunds if necessary."

Sonia frowned. "But…"

"Garrett, are you ready to go?" Kara said.

Garrett stepped up smoothly, twirling his keys around his finger. "Your chariot awaits, Sis."

She called a goodbye to her mother and the dogs and hurried to the car.

Buckled up, she accepted a travel cup of hot tea from Garrett and thanked him fervently. Though she had changed into dry clothes, she was still chilled through and through. They drove up and over the mountain, and she couldn't keep the memory of the paintball attack on the van from surfacing.

Garrett gave no outward sign that he was anything but relaxed, but she caught his surreptitious peeks at the rear and side-view mirrors. Nothing came at them but a spatter of wet pine needles blown from the trees.

She was almost finished with the tea when he finally spoke up.

"You sounded like you were taking charge back there with Sonia."

"Someone had to do it."

"Could be Ree isn't up for Pioneer Day, and with Beau, er, grappling with a brain injury…"

"Garrett, no one should cancel anything without Ree's permission, or at least a meeting between Beau and the employees. It's not Sonia's place to make decisions."

He flashed her a surprised smile. "Know what?"

"What?"

"I completely agree. I like this version of you."

"What version?"

"The kind that doesn't hesitate to speak her mind. I think Beau admires it too."

*Beau?* Heat crept up her throat, and she couldn't think of how to respond, so she remained silent for the drive and was relieved when they made it to the hospital.

Garrett walked her to the hallway, where they

found Beau pacing. He glanced at her—through her, actually—then his gaze darted back. She smiled and waved, watching him scan for a couple of seconds before recognition dawned across his face.

"Kara," he said. "Thanks for coming. You too, Garrett."

"No problem," Garrett said. "How's your mother?"

"Unconscious, relatively stable, considering. They're treating her for hypothermia with hemodialysis and intravenous fluids. She has mild frostbite, some pretty bad bruising, and the most worrying is a concussion from a wound on the back of her head."

Kara's breath caught. "From falling?"

"Good question." Beau rubbed his chin. "Too close to home for me."

Kara knew he was thinking about what had happened to him seven months before. A blow struck from someone in the shadows... "You think someone attacked her like they did to you?"

"I don't know."

Garrett's phone buzzed and he stepped away to take the call.

"How are you doing, Beau?" Kara asked.

"Hanging in there. I'd breathe a lot easier if Mom would wake up, but the doctors say that may not happen for several days."

Sheriff Franco emerged from Ree's hospital room. His uniform was wrinkled, and there was a smudge of mud on one knee as if he'd fallen.

The sheriff pointed to his badge. "Franco."

Beau flinched. "I know. I can read your name tag."

"Right. Thanks for telling me about the face recognition thing. Explains a lot."

Kara was relieved that the sheriff was briefed. It had probably taken a toll on Beau's ego to admit it.

"Did you find any evidence to explain what happened?"

"No, but my officers found this." Franco offered an envelope. "Already photographed it, but it doesn't appear to be related in any way to what happened, so I figured I'd do you a solid and turn it over. It was in her back pocket. And it's, uh, due soon."

Beau opened it. "A utility bill. It's a big one. Due end of the month. She's counting on…" Kara saw him go taut as the date sank in. It was Friday afternoon.

"Pioneer Day," she finished.

Franco frowned. "With everything that's gone down, maybe it's not the wisest decision to go forward with that."

Beau frowned. "Why not? Because Mom's hurt? I can—"

Franco cut him off. "The initial evidence indicates that she was moved to the location where you found her."

Kara gasped.

Beau's mouth dropped open. "Moved?"

"Yes."

The image of someone hauling Beau's injured mother and dumping her near the river made Kara nauseous. What had she done to earn such deadly hatred?

Franco stared at Beau. "Reminiscent of the Thanksgiving situation, isn't it?"

Kara's nerves cinched tighter. "Beau's enemy is back?"

Franco continued to look directly at Beau. "It would appear so, and until we figure out what their vendetta is against Beau and the O'Connor family, everyone in the proximity could be a target."

*Everyone.*

Kara felt Beau looking at her.

Beau had come home, but he'd stepped into a cyclone of violence.

And so had she.

*Everyone in the proximity could be a target.*

Beau's enemy, the one he'd known was out there since that night in November, wasn't satisfied with injuring Beau and taking his career…

he or she had gone after his mother. Fury tangled with a strange relief that Franco now had come around to fully believing him, but at what cost? Acid rose in his throat. Emotions could wait. Main objective first. "Mom needs protection."

"I've arranged for her room to be monitored, only preapproved visitors allowed." Franco pointed to a tiny black box at the end of the hallway. "And we can survey the feed from that hospital camera from the station."

"But I really think with you and your mom a target, the Pioneer Day…" Franco started.

"It's not an option to cancel. I'll handle it myself. Whatever it takes." He tapped the envelope. "She needs the money."

Kara looked pained. "I… I need to tell the sheriff something in confidence."

Beau stared at her. "About my mom's situation?"

She bit her lower lip. "I'm not sure it pertains, but I have to tell him in case it's relevant."

His jaw tightened. "If it's about Mom, I have a right to know."

Kara let out a low breath. "I'm sorry, Beau, but she asked me not to tell you."

Now he was downright gobsmacked. His mom was keeping secrets from him? Kara's earlier remarks about the property and his return rose to the surface. "This is something to do with the hatchery, isn't it?"

She kept her focus on Sheriff Franco. "I was asked to keep the matter private."

The sheriff looked from Kara to Beau and back again. "With Ree's health situation undetermined, it'd be best to tell both of us at this point, Ms. Wolfe. It won't go further than this conversation unless it needs to."

She took a deep breath, fingers intertwined as she prepared herself. "Ree asked me to arrange the sale of the hatchery property."

Beau rocked back on his heels. "Why wouldn't she tell me that?"

"I'm not certain, she didn't discuss her reasons. I know she wasn't aware that you were planning to come back permanently."

"When did she arrange for the sale?" he demanded.

"Two weeks ago."

His mind reeled. "Did she tell you why she was selling?"

"No."

"You don't even have a guess?" He shook his head as an awful thought crept in, and he could barely get the words out. "Was it because my brain is scrambled and she had some need to provide for me?"

She reached for him, stopping short. "I'm sure it wasn't that, Beau. I…"

He shook his head, stopping her. Anger simmered along with something worse. Hurt.

Maybe he didn't have a right to be upset at Kara for keeping secrets, not as though he'd treated her like a treasured pal, but he was irate anyway, torn by her secrecy, pained at his mother's.

He turned to Franco, spine ramrod straight, refusing to look at Kara. "All right then. Now that you know the big secret, could it be that someone doesn't want her to sell?"

Franco frowned. "Who would that be? Besides you, I mean? And why would that have precipitated these attacks? Recent or past?"

He had no answer.

The sheriff considered. "I'll take that information into account and see what I can dig up. In the meantime, about Pioneer Day…"

"It's happening," he snapped. "Like I said, I'll handle it."

"All right. Be in touch soon."

Franco left and Beau stood shaking his head, staring at the length of the empty corridor. The silence thickened to the point of smothering.

"I'm sorry," Kara said. "Truly. I didn't want to keep it from you."

"But you did." Anger bubbled out, spilling his

wrath onto her. "Maybe if you'd told me this before, Mom and I would have talked and none of this would've happened." His rage struck at her, but she straightened and looked right back at him.

"Beau, I know you're upset, but what happened to your mother was not because I didn't disclose—"

"You can't be sure of that."

Kara stared him down. "She was missing when you showed up in town…without telling me, I might add. I was honoring her wishes, by the way."

"You must have been eager to take the listing though," he snapped. "Restarting your real estate career?" He knew as he spat out the words he was being unfair, but he couldn't stop himself. It felt like the hammer in the nail of his coffin, his mom selling the hatchery in secret.

Her chin quivered, but she kept her tone steady. "Yes, it was a great way to get my foot in the door again, but I would have helped her even if it didn't benefit me. I hope you know me well enough to realize that."

Her strong rebuttal surprised him and took the sting out of his rage. He looked at the tears forming in her eyes, and he knew she'd been agonized about keeping his mother's decision from him. His remark had been uncalled for, unmerited.

This was Henny Penny, and it was his mother's property to do with as she saw fit.

*Two deep breaths. Keep your cool, Marine.*

"You're right, I do know that, Kara. That was a low blow. I can't exactly ream you out for not keeping me informed when I basically skipped town without a word to you. I apologize."

She was silent a moment, then she smiled. "I accept. And I am sorry to have kept a secret from you."

She was sorry, that much was clear. And even after he'd dismissed her from his life, she'd tried to help his mother. He'd live with the hurt. He cleared his throat to drive away the awkward silence. "I'm going to see Mom. Would you like to come?"

She nodded.

They checked in with the security guard before he pushed open the door and allowed Kara in first. She hesitated, stumbling almost, her hand pressed to her stomach as if she were stifling a pain.

Instantly he was at her elbow. "What's wrong?"

"Nothing," she whispered as they approached. The woman lying before them was so small in the big hospital bed, her short hair wispy and flyaway without her customary knit cap. A lump formed in his throat as he gripped the bedrail and willed his brain to catch up.

*This is your mother...your mother.* But his desperate yearning for recognition was not satisfied as he stared at her. He closed his eyes, and his heart began to rip in half until Kara's hand covered his, guiding his fingers to his mother's.

She cupped his over hers and squeezed. "You know her."

And his fingertips recognized what his brain couldn't, the hands that had held him, comforted him, built a business, buried her husband, his father. The crooked pinky from a childhood injury, the skin toughened by hard work and California sunshine. His mother. He didn't realize that he was crying until Kara handed him a tissue.

Embarrassed by his fraying control, Beau tried to get himself together as he talked. "It's gonna be fine, Mom. Don't worry. Doc says you'll be okay after a while, and I'm going to handle Pioneer Day."

She remained still, eyes closed, without so much as a twitch to indicate she'd heard. As he sat by his mother's bedside, chatting for all he was worth about everything and nothing, Kara drifted in and out of the room, on the phone with her family, bringing coffee and a sandwich for her and Beau to share. They stayed until the nurse politely pointed out that the visiting hours were over.

He kissed his mother's cool cheek, taking one

more long look to burn her facial details into his
psyche, even though he knew it was a useless effort. Tomorrow when he came, his recognition
would be a blank, as if his memory had been
sanded smooth.

In a daze, he walked beside Kara to Big Blue.
"I'll drive you back to Whisper Valley."

She nodded. "It'll be a quick stop, just long
enough to grab my things and the dogs. I'll drive
myself back to the hatchery, but I'd like to follow you in case the paintball guy has reloaded
his supplies."

He stopped. "Kara, I can handle everything.
You stay at the ranch."

"I'm going to help you with Pioneer Day."

"I don't need help."

"Yes, you do."

Again he felt the brush of hurt. "I don't need
your pity or guilt."

"Beau, I have neither of those things. Once
upon a time we were dear friends, and no matter
what's happened, I'm going to act like we still
are until you come around."

"I..." He looked from the sky to her to the
sky again. Until he came around? Had he actually ever stopped thinking of her? Even when it
hurt? "You heard Franco. It's dangerous. There's
an enemy at work we can't yet identify."

"I've been thinking about that, actually. When

we have free time, Millie can sniff around, maybe find your mother's original trail where she was wounded. That might lead us to some answers or motives."

And to a myriad of new dangers.

He grabbed her hand and squeezed. "I appreciate it, I really do, but I'm not going to have you risk your safety."

She patted his fingers, then let them go. "I've got two dogs and I don't intend to do anything foolish. I'll stay in your mother's room, if you're still okay with that, and there will be plenty of people around while we prep for Pioneer Day."

His last card was a desperate one. "Your brothers will never go along with it."

She laughed. "They're not the boss of me. And neither are you. I'm going to see this through, Beau O'Connor, for your mother's sake." Her voice wobbled. "I love her, and I'm going to pitch in until she can take over the watch herself."

He felt again the sparks dancing along his nerves at the lift of her chin, the gleam of determination, her pure love for his mother. With Kara by his side, he might actually be able to pull off Pioneer Day. But relieved as he was to have someone dedicated to helping him keep the hatchery afloat, fear tugged at his stomach.

His enemy wasn't finished.

Not by a mile.

# NINE

Kara expected a battle, and she got one after she announced her plans to stay at the hatchery. When Chase saw that Kara wouldn't reconsider, he was ready to pack a bag and accompany her, but a call for the Security Hounds team required him and Garrett to head for the mountains to find a missing hiker.

Beth would need to deploy along with Garrett and Chase to coordinate the team. None of them were pleased at Kara's decision, and all stated they would be hustling to the hatchery as soon as their search wrapped. The Wolfe family was a pack, all right, and they weren't comfortable with her leaving the safety of their den.

But life wasn't a safe adventure at all, she'd learned. And hiding from risk wasn't what the Lord wanted from her.

Stephanie and Vance were away on a trip to evaluate some rescued bloodhounds, and Roman was attending yet another class with his dog

Wally, who steadfastly refused to be trained in whatever the dog deemed unnecessary. To Roman's deep mortification, Wally had already swiped an entire platter of hot dogs from the event lunchroom.

Her brothers ended the visit with frighteningly serious looks at Beau.

Beau shot his chin up, eyes a blaze of sapphire. "Not my wishes either, guys, but I will make sure nothing happens to her." He appeared every bit as determined as her brothers, standing tall and tense as if he were guiding his assault vehicle into enemy territory.

Finally, she got her car loaded and took off, following Big Blue. The drive was uneventful, and the dogs appeared content to be on the move again. Phil was the kind of canine that never fully settled anywhere, and Millie wasn't picky about her surroundings as long as she had a soft blanket and lots of human affection.

Kara was relieved they made it through the twistiest part of the trail before sunset. Beau insisted on carrying her bag upstairs while she set up the dogs' bowls in the kitchen attached to the downstairs office.

Stomach growling, she wished she'd thought to stop for groceries. It felt odd, now that she was here, sorting through domestic details like meals.

But why should it? Beau was merely a friend and she was helping out. That was all.

A rap on the door brought Beau jogging down-stairs before she made it out of the kitchen. "I got it." He was taking his promise to her brothers seriously.

Natalie Clark stood on the doorstep, her horse behind her, nosing at the grass that had sprouted around the bird feeder. The porch light picked up the concern on her face, the parentheses carved around her mouth.

Beau greeted her and invited her in. Kara wasn't sure if he recognized Natalie, but his tone was convincing. Kara wondered how many people knew of Beau's condition.

"Hello, Natalie," Kara said, in case Beau needed a name to put with the face.

"Hi. I came to see…" She looked around the office space. "I wanted to ask about Ree." She held up two large canning jars, the contents sloshing inside. "I made some soup for you and your mom. Ree likes my chicken noodle. It's all from scratch, even the noodles."

Beau accepted the jars. "Thank you. That was very thoughtful."

"She's still in the hospital?"

"Yes. Not responsive but her vitals are stable."

"Oh." Natalie's voice dropped. "She's going to be okay, right? I can't believe she was lying out there all that time hurting and alone. I was sure she'd just gone off on a delivery and forgotten to tell anyone about it. I never, ever, thought it would come to this."

"They're taking great care of her," Kara put in.

Natalie declined when Beau gestured for her to sit.

"I have horses to feed." She fisted her hands on her hips. "It's unbelievable that Ree's not here. She is always bursting with energy and determination since I've known her. Even when your dad died, it didn't stop her from managing it all." Natalie cocked her head. "Do you think she was hiking and fell?"

"It's unclear." Beau paused. "More likely she was attacked."

Natalie's mouth dropped open. "I can't believe that. What would be the point? She didn't have piles of money lying around. She counted every last nickel. There's nothing here worth stealing." She chewed her lip. "A random attack? Someone high or drunk?"

"We'll find out." Hard-edged determination cut through his words.

"I'll help in any way I'm able," Natalie said. "Can I go see her?"

"Not right now. Security's tight." Beau promised to let her know when his mother was receiving visitors as he opened the door to usher

her out. At the last minute Natalie pivoted on her heel.

"Oh my gosh. Pioneer Day. What are you going to do?"

"Carry on," Beau said, arms folded across his chest, eyes narrowed. "Why wouldn't we? Kara's here to help."

Natalie sighed. "Good. It's exactly what your mom would want, isn't it? But...keep alert."

Kara looked closer at the woman.

"For what in particular?" Beau said, his gaze suddenly sharp. "Do you suspect who might be behind the attacks?"

Natalie's gaze drifted to the employee cabins facing the office. "I don't know. Just seems like Ree would have been cautious if a stranger approached her, so maybe..."

"Was it someone she knew?" Kara pressed.

Natalie shrugged. "I don't want to believe it. I'm no detective, for sure. Anyway, good night."

Beau closed the door.

Kara went to heat up a pan of Natalie's chicken soup. "Who does she suspect?"

"I don't know, but there was definitely an undertone."

Kara fed Millie and Phil and served up the bowls of Natalie's offering for the humans. Beau offered a heartfelt grace and they devoured the soup, a rich broth with tender vegetables and chunks of chicken.

Beau insisted on doing the dishes and she acquiesced. Her body throbbed with fatigue, as well as the bumps and bruises she'd acquired when the log bridge failed. She wandered to the window, looking out on the darkened hatchery property to the right, the employee housing straight across, all the curtains drawn. Mentally she scrolled through the arduous day, finally allowing herself to experience the feelings that had swamped her at the hospital.

The smell of disinfectant, the squeak of rubber soles echoing along twisted corridors, the beep and chirp of monitoring equipment…it was all injected in her senses like some indelible dye. She closed her eyes against a swell of dizziness. Millie pawed her leg and Phil scooted closer.

Beau dropped the dish towel and hurried to her. "What's wrong?"

She tried to explain it away, but he wasn't buying it.

"You had that same look in the hospital today." He led her to the sofa, where he sat next to her, and Millie and Phil took up posts at her feet.

"I was…remembering. It kind of came back when we visited your mom. Sort of a post-traumatic reaction to what happened with Kyle, I think. I felt it also when I stayed with my mom in the hospital after her back surgery."

He caressed her fingers. "I know that was a terrible situation with Kyle."

"Terrible, yes, but there were blessings in it too." She swallowed. "I wish we'd been married, but Kyle kept putting it off. Some of it was due to his silly pride. 'I'm going to stand and watch you walk down the aisle to me, Kara,' he'd say and he insisted I buy the dress. As time wore on, I offered to arrange a ceremony at his bedside, but—" she blinked hard "—the end came faster than we all thought it would."

"Oh, Kara." He pressed her fingers to his cheek. "Is there anything I can do? Now, I mean?"

She started to make something up to deflect, but instead she sought his gaze. "I spent a lot of time in the hospital with Kyle. It was lonely and frightening, and every day I braced for bad news. I didn't realize until later how much it affected me."

Beau dropped his head. "I should have been there with you more."

"You were there, as often as you could be when you were stateside."

He shook his head. "I meant being emotionally present, to take care of you."

She swallowed. "You tried."

"Not enough. We both know that. I kept myself apart in some ways."

He had. "Why, Beau?"

Now he raised his blue eyes to hers, and she knew whatever came after would be the truth.

"I didn't want… It didn't feel right to step into the middle of what you had with Kyle, especially not when you were losing him. Now I'm beginning to realize I shouldn't have been focused on what *I* was feeling. Kyle was dying and you were suffering, and that should have taken precedence over my discomfort. I'm sorry."

She should offer placating words to ease his distress. But something else came out. "Me too. I could have used a shoulder to cry on. I had to be strong for Kyle and his sister and parents, but I was grieving too." A tear trickled hot down her cheek, and he reached up and brushed it away.

She felt his warmth, the sweetness of his touch. Who moved to close the gap between them? She wasn't sure, but suddenly their lips met, and she was enveloped by a breathtaking sensation of comfort, sorrow and peace all at once. It lasted only a moment before he released her.

"I'm…" he said. "I'm not sure why I did that."

She felt a stab of sadness at his regret. "Emotions running high," she said softly. "I won't read anything into it, don't worry."

And she'd try not to, but her feelings cascaded

in unexpected circles, and the shared space felt suddenly small, the silence awkward. She excused herself and took the dogs upstairs.

*Put it out of your mind.* Whatever had happened between them was a source of discomfort for Beau, and he didn't need any more pressure. She settled Millie and Phil and climbed into Ree's small bed.

Sleep eluded her, so she read a textbook about the real estate business, which finally allowed her to nod off. It seemed only minutes later that her eyes popped open again when she heard Phil stirring.

Kara looked over to find him on his feet, staring at her. It would have been terrifying if she didn't know the dog so well.

"Do you need to go out, boy?"

Millie yawned and shook her ears, climbing heavily to her paws, ever the good sport.

Kara sighed, the clock taunting her with the time—3:30 a.m. "Why do you always decide on going out when I've finally managed to fall asleep?"

She grabbed her phone and eased out of bed. They tiptoed past Beau's room and listened to him snoring softly. She'd heard him pacing the office floor at two, when she'd woken, remembering she hadn't applied Millie's eye ointment. They'd agreed to be up at five sharp to plunge into the festival prep, but Phil couldn't wait another hour and a half for an outside break. She'd allow a quick pit stop directly out front on the small grassy area, no wandering the property at night. Beau wouldn't approve of her decision, but she could not bring herself to rouse him after a grueling day that led right into an even more stressful one. Phone in her pocket, she slipped shoes on her bare feet, grateful for the leggings and warm shirt she'd worn to bed in Ree's chilly room.

As the three of them crept down the staircase, she thought about what she'd told Beau in the hospital. *Once upon a time we were dear friends, and no matter what's happened, I'm going to act like we still are until you come around.* Something about the statement chimed a false note.

"Friend." The word did not fully capture her feelings for Beau. Was he more than that to her? Had her feelings swelled from simple affection? The way she'd felt when he'd kissed her certainly led to that conclusion. She shook away the notion. He would never allow himself to be more than a friend, she realized, because of Kyle. The thought saddened her, because Kyle had only ever wanted Kara to have whatever gave her fulfillment and happiness.

But that wouldn't be a relationship with Beau, and she'd have to accept that. Friends, she told herself firmly, would be enough of a blessing.

The dogs' collars had no metal parts to jingle, so they glided silently onto the ground floor and she unlocked and eased open the front door. Leaving it ajar, she stepped out into the crisp air that immediately chilled her. She'd kept a leash on Millie since the dog could not be trusted if there was a rodent in the vicinity. Phil stuck close to Millie's side as they roamed the mushy grass area.

The employee residences were quiet and dark, except for a light shining from behind the closed curtains at Vince's place.

Phil cocked an ear at the darkened shrubs growing haphazardly between the office grounds and the residences. The dog's body tensed.

Goose bumps swept up her back. She stood frozen, gripping Millie's leash. If Phil lost interest, she'd know everything was okay. He didn't. Instead, the scruff of his neck rose in spiky prickles. Probably an animal, but she wasn't going to stay and investigate.

Immediately, she tugged Millie back toward the house. Phil ignored her command to follow. He barked at something she could not see. She turned toward the door, scurrying back toward safety, Millie confused about why Phil wasn't following them.

Two strides from the front step she caught an image in the front window of the office.

A face reflected in the glass. Someone standing behind her.

Watching them.

Watching her.

Beau hit the bottom step when Phil let out his third bark. The first one had brought him leaping out of bed, jamming on boots, and the second pounding down the stairs. His heart slammed so hard against his ribs it felt like taking enemy fire. *Kara...outside...?* He didn't ponder the why or how. The only thing on his mind was grabbing her up and carrying her to safety, if necessary. The door was open, and he plunged across the threshold. He almost collided with Kara on the porch, her face dead white in the gloom. He clutched her forearms and felt her trembling, her panicked breaths.

"There's...someone..." She was holding Millie on a leash, which was tangled around her leg. Phil barked at full volume in the yard. "I saw a reflection in the front window."

"Inside." He propelled her into the office with Millie keeping pace.

"But Phil won't obey you, I have to be there to..."

He didn't let her finish, simply moved her and Millie farther into the house. "Lock the door."

He'd grabbed his handgun and flashlight on

the way out, and now he gripped them tightly. Phil continued to make a ruckus, darting looks from Beau to the shadows. Beau hoped Phil would recognize him as a neutral party at least, if not a friend. Beau peered into the darkness, the cloud-cloaked moon not helping his recon. He checked the angles. Kara had seen an intruder reflected in the window, so they would likely have been positioned in the narrow passage between the two residences. He flicked on the flashlight. The beam caught nothing but leaves and overgrown shrubs quivering in the breeze.

Phil ceased barking, shook himself and backed up a step but remained alert.

Beau was about to creep down the passage between the two employee cabins when Vince's door opened. The grizzled hair and slouched shoulders confirmed for Beau that it was his mom's longtime employee. He was dressed in the same clothes from that morning, a shotgun held tightly in his hands.

Phil barked.

"What?" Vince demanded.

"Someone was out here. Was it you?"

"Just what exactly would I be doing outside at this hour?" Vince snarled. "Talking to the fish?"

"I don't know," Beau snapped back. "You're not dressed for sleeping. Want to explain that?"

Vince bridled. "I don't have to explain that. Are you accusing me of something, kid?"

*Kid? Be calm.* Inflaming the situation wasn't going to get him any usable intel. Beau didn't fire off a reply before the door of the second structure opened to reveal another man. Beau did a quick analysis. Middle-aged, thinning hair, goatee, long fingers. John Partridge. He had a bathrobe pulled across his middle, feet covered in thick socks.

His eyes were wide as he looked from Beau to Vince. "What's all the noise?"

Phil barked some more at the newcomer and John recoiled a step.

"Phil, return," he heard Kara call out sternly. She had technically followed his directive and stayed inside, but he hadn't specifically told her not to open the window. Phil skewered Vince and John with a suspicious glare before he returned to the house, leaving the humans to their own problems.

Good. Kara and Millie would be well protected and he could focus on sorting out what had happened.

"There's an intruder on the property apparently." There was a hint of sarcasm as Vince shouldered his shotgun.

Beau watched both of them closely. "Yes.

Looking in the front window when Kara went out with the dogs."

"Really? That makes no sense," John said.

"I'll check the cameras, but they don't cover this area," Vince said.

True. They were installed only for research purposes and focused tightly on the stock ponds and the rearing channels. He made a note to install more to track the comings and goings of the main building.

"I'll check around. Whoever it was had to have run off between your houses."

Beau didn't want company, but Vince and John prepared to follow him, John ducking inside for shoes. They picked their way over the spongy ground as they searched for evidence of an intruder. With the wind blowing and the weak light, there was no sign anyone had passed that way. Beau intended to check closer for footprints when daylight came. Without company.

"You sure it was a person, not an animal? We've got a mountain lion around," Vince said. "Natalie spotted one last week."

But Kara had said "someone" not "something," and there was no way she would have mistaken a human predator for the feline variety. "I'll check around in the morning."

"Should I call the police?" John said.

"I'll fill them in." Beau walked back with

Vince and John in tow. "Sorry to awaken you all." He glanced at John's place, the rear bedroom dark, curtains in place. "Your wife's a heavy sleeper? She didn't hear the dog barking and our talking?"

John nodded. "Sonia can sleep through a jet landing in the backyard. Wish I could. I was in the living room looking for the cookies she hides from me when I heard the ruckus." He glanced at Vince. "You up too at this hour? Can't sleep?"

Vince shrugged. "Got a lot to do tomorrow. Night." He spun on his heel and vanished into his unit, followed by John a moment later.

Beau jogged back to the office. Was someone lying? Did Vince's refusal to explain why he was awake or Sonia's ability to sleep through the tumult hint at their guilt? Kara let him in. She'd been watching from the window, perhaps listening too, and her cell phone was ready in case of trouble. Millie was busily licking Phil.

"You okay?" Beau slid the window closed and locked it.

She nodded. "Scared me, is all. Before you launch into a tirade, I know I shouldn't have taken the dogs out by myself, but you were so tired. I didn't want to wake you."

"Kara, I could be dead on my feet, and I'd still want you to wake me. Promise me right now you're not going to leave this building again without my knowledge." He hoped he'd kept the fear out of his voice, the abject terror he felt that someone could have hurt her.

She tucked her hair behind her ear. "Well, I…"

He shook his head. "Promise. Now."

"I promise."

He blew out a breath and told her of his plans to check the property again in the daylight and the information he'd gotten from Vince and John. "And Sonia didn't wake up at all." He paused. "The reflection you saw. Man or woman, could you tell?"

She shook her head. "I only got a quick glance, the hair was covered. They might have been wearing a hoodie. Not sure about height, but it probably won't help anyway. Vince, John and Sonia are all similarly built. There's no reason to assume it was an employee, is there?"

"Anyone could hike onto the property, it's true. Long walk in the dark though."

"But for what purpose? Why would someone be sneaking around?" Her eyes locked on his face. "It's like the night you were hurt, isn't it? Someone out there with a motive that was never uncovered."

She shivered, and he realized the room was cold and she must be freezing. He grabbed the old, worn quilt and draped it around her shoulders, tucking the ends together under her chin.

"I'll call Franco before I turn in again. And I'm keeping my door cracked so I can hear if you need anything."

"Or if I sneak out?"

He arched a brow.

"Kidding," she said with a rueful smile. "I'll try to sleep for the entire two hours until we wake up to start our day."

He kept up the stern tone. "If I'm not in the kitchen when you come down, wait inside for me."

"You'll be looking for footprints?"

"That's one thing working in our favor. The ground is wet, and there's no way for someone to walk through that passage without leaving a trail."

"I wonder what would have happened if Phil hadn't alerted me." She looked down, a shudder rippling her shoulders.

He reached out and caressed her cheek. "Remember your promise, okay?"

Her smile, scared but undaunted, got right inside of him.

The thought of someone watching Kara, stalking her, turned his vision all red and misty.

Another threat added to the pile.

But this one was much closer to home.

# TEN

Kara woke to her alarm, bleary and sand-eyed. It took her a moment to realize there was muffled shouting coming from downstairs. Her stomach flipped. What now? Had Beau been attacked while he searched for prints?

She sprinted downstairs, the dogs galloping at her heels until they reached the living room, where she yanked the curtains back and peeked outside. The porch lights shone on the ground around the office, gleaming off inches of standing water. As she gaped, Beau appeared, tall rubber boots rippling the surface.

Vince splashed by, clutching a wrench. John and Sonia followed a moment later with buckets. She slid the window open.

"Beau, what's happened?"

He blinked, bringing her into focus. His expression was pure fury, eyes blazing blue fire. Did he recognize her from her voice? she wondered.

"The water pump that feeds the raceways failed. It flooded the whole area. We'll get it contained in a few."

Her thoughts whirled as she slid the window closed. A flood…how convenient. The passageway between the houses where the intruder might have left prints was now a sodden mess. There would be no way to observe any signs that might lead to the perpetrator. But if someone was covering their tracks, did that point to it being one of the employees?

She dressed, tended the dogs and waited, her thoughts twisting and turning until she heard the grumble of a pump coming to life. Slowly the water level began to recede. It was a few minutes after 6:00 a.m. when Beau squelched across the muddy ground, dumped his boots on the porch and entered.

His gaze roved her face. As she handed him a mug of coffee, he looked hard at her hands as she cupped them around his. He offered a tired smile. "Recognized you in only a few seconds this time. Beating this prosopagnosia beast, right?"

She chafed his cold fingers. "Learning to live with it and that takes heart."

His cheeks flushed, and he continued to stare at their joined hands. How odd, she thought, that humans invest too much in a face. Beau was adapting by cataloging other clues, and she was proud of him for it. She suddenly realized she'd been holding on for too long, and she let go and poured her own cup of coffee. "What happened to the pump?"

"Hard to say. Yes, the bolts were rusty, but they could have had help." With a groan, he rubbed his face. "Mom would have been on it way before I was. She knows every sound of this place. She'd have heard the pump acting up as soon as it failed. Vince texted my phone this morning."

"How is she today, Beau? Any word?"

He drank another slug of coffee. "I called just before Vince messaged. She's still unconscious. Stable but not showing signs of rousing. I'll go this afternoon to visit if we can get clear."

"I'll go with you if you'd like me to."

He smiled. "I'd love that. I didn't want to pressure."

"Why would I feel pressured? Haven't we known each other for decades?"

"Yep. Since we were young teens who thought we knew all the answers to life's questions. I thought we'd always be best buds—you, me and Kyle, but everything changed when Kyle invited you to the prom first..." He broke off.

She blinked. "First? You mean *you* were going to ask me?"

His wandering gaze flicked over everything

in the room but her. "Uh, yeah. But you know, Kyle was always quicker on his feet than me."

"You wanted to date me."

He gaped at her now. "Of course I did. Who in their right mind wouldn't want to go out with you?"

Her? The slightly nerdy girl who rescued earth-worms from drowning, didn't go to the cool parties or wear fashionable clothes? "Did Kyle know that?" she said finally.

"Nah."

"You didn't ever talk it over with him?" Suddenly the strange distance that had crept in between them started to make sense.

"No."

"Why in the world not?"

"Some things men just don't discuss. You were with Kyle and you were great together. End of story."

She rolled her eyes and heaved out a breath. "Forgive me for saying so, but men are silly sometimes."

He chuckled. "Yeah. I'd have to say that describes my actions where you're concerned. I'm a confident person, or at least I was, in my physical abilities, my job, sure of myself, but when it came to you…" He shrugged. "For some reason I'm dim-witted where you…where women are concerned."

She tried to absorb it all. Beau and Kyle both wanted to date her, and Beau hadn't said a peep about it to either one of them. "But things should have been so much easier. We were the three musketeers, we could have stayed…" She was going to say, "just the same," but in that moment she knew it wouldn't have been possible for Beau to maintain the level of closeness to her and Kyle that he'd had before. Something had gotten between them, his feelings for her, the "man code" perhaps. And she hadn't had a clue. "I didn't realize you felt awkward about it. I wish you'd told me."

"Admitting I couldn't handle being around my buddy and his girl? That'd be weak. And I didn't want to make anyone feel uncomfortable."

His expression rendered him boyish, the tender, affectionate young man she'd known and cared for deeply. She laughed, reached out and squeezed his forearm. "Beau O'Connor, you're still my friend, dim-witted or not."

A relieved smile drifted over his face. "That's the best piece of news I've had in forever."

"And you've forgiven me for not telling you about the property sale?"

"Not your fault. I have some ground to cover with Mom, but that can all wait. I've got my friend back, and I feel like God has lifted the weight off my shoulders that I've been hauling for a long time."

Before she could second-guess her impulse, she leaned in to kiss him on the cheek, but he turned and her lips brushed his.

The tingle that passed through was warm as a summer day. Was it more with Beau than friendship? No. Friends only. Partners in keeping the hatchery afloat. Allies. Whatever else she felt must be put away for now. He hadn't moved—he froze there—staring at her until he lunged for a notepad and pen on the counter.

"You know what the best part of deployment was? The pens. In Afghanistan, we delivered humanitarian assistance to children. Gets real cold there in the winter, so they needed blankets, clothes, shoes. And we distributed backpacks with school supplies. The kids were so excited for pens. Every time I'd go through town, they'd come running. 'Mister Soldier, can I have a pen?' I used to carry as many as I could cram into my pockets." He shook his head, a wistful smile on his face.

"They say it's mightier than the sword," she teased.

He stuck the pen behind his ear. "We weren't allowed to hand out swords."

They both laughed until the clock chimed.

"Is it seven already?" Beau groaned.

"Yes, soldier, it is, so let's get the lead out and start prepping for the festival. Tomorrow's going to be here before you know it." She thrust a sandwich at him she'd made. "Fuel up while you make your list."

He chuckled. "Copy that, Henny Penny."

"I helped myself to bread and such. It's a fried egg sandwich, a Wolfe family classic."

He took a massive bite. "Way better than the protein shake I was planning to down."

"I'll take that as a compliment."

A shadow crossed his eyes. "Franco should be here later, but you'll stay close today, right? No moving out of my sight, even if I can't remember who you are for any length of time?"

"Copy that," she echoed, but she caught his gaze and held it. "But you do remember who I am, Beau." She pointed to his chest. "Here, where it matters."

His lips quivered and he took a breath. "Going to be a long day, but if it's a safe one, I won't complain."

Would it be safe? While Beau made notes of things that needed doing when they returned, her gaze drifted to the window. The water had almost completely ebbed away along with whatever evidence they might have collected. Pump failure or sabotage? She set aside the worry as they plunged into the to-do list.

Beau hustled across the property. He hastened to the picnic area to unload the rows of stacked folding chairs around the small amphitheater while she focused on prepping the craft tables where the kids would make posters to cheer on their participant in the fish races. A couple hours later, with everything in place, she covered the tables with a cloth and clamped it down. Her phone rang with a call from her mother. She provided an update on the intruder and the failed pump. "What's the status there?"

"Boys found the missing hiker, injured but alive. There'll be a couple more hours waiting for the rescue personnel to transport the victim down from the mountains. While I'm waiting, I'll work on researching the employees and Natalie. Who does your gut tell you might be an enemy?"

"Vince is pretty hostile, for reasons unknown. And…"

"And what?"

"This might sound odd, but my first choice would be someone who isn't even here, supposedly. Rocklin Clark, Natalie's husband. He despised Beau, but he's in Europe, she told me."

"He could be lying, regarding his whereabouts, or maybe he came back without her knowledge. It's also possible that he could have hired someone here to do his dirty work. It bears looking into."

Kara frowned. "What would be the motive? What would he gain? He's moved on from the area and his marriage."

"Some people never really get over their hatred, do they?"

That statement awakened a little thrill of fear.

"We'll be there as soon as we can, and I'll look into connections in the meantime," her mother said. "Be safe."

Kara signed off and moved to the next task, which was arranging supplies in the barbecue pit area for the hot dog roast. Beau waved at her from the ladder. He'd now moved on to stringing lights. Though he was busy with his own tasks, she knew he hadn't let her drift out of his line of sight. Why did that thought warm her?

*Because you're friends again.* But it was in a different way than when Kyle was alive.

She took a break to offer the dogs snacks and an ear rub. Phil stood a pace in front of Millie as Sonia arrived with her arms full.

Sonia frowned. "Your dog doesn't like me."

"He doesn't have a large circle of friends, but he's not barking at you, at least."

She rolled her eyes, slid a box on the table and yawned. Glimmers of silver hair were intermingled with her blond French braids. "My day started way too early with that flooding business." Her eyes were assessing. "I heard Vince say it was intentional, the peeping Tom trying to cover their tracks. Is that what you think?"

"I don't know. What's your take?"

She yawned again. "I have no idea, but if someone is sabotaging the property, I wish they'd do it in daylight hours."

Kara thought the comment tasteless. This was Beau and Ree's livelihood, and the flood was a setback, no matter what the cause. "Sheriff Franco will work on it. Hopefully Ree won't have to worry about any more incidents when she comes home."

Sonia batted away a fly. "Is she going to take up where she left off? Working on the trail and all that?"

"You don't think it's a good idea?"

Sonia shrugged. "I've hiked up that trail and the view's great, but it needs a ton of improvement, for sure. If it were me, I wouldn't bother. The visitor count may increase, but how does that actually translate to profit for the hatchery? Unless you're going to charge a usage fee or something, and from what I know of Ree, she isn't going to do that." She shrugged again. "She's soft."

Kara didn't agree. Ree's tender heart didn't mean she couldn't run a business. "We haven't had a chance to talk much. What exactly do you do for the hatchery?"

"Handle the social media and website, mostly."

Her tone was less than enthusiastic. "Not your life's work?"

Sonia laughed. "You could say that. I'm a marine biologist. I've worked up and down the state. That's how I met John, actually. He taught at a postgraduate seminar about hatchery water circulation systems. Honestly, I thought the subject matter was a bore, but the other classes at the conference were full. Right before we got married last year, the funding for my job dried up, so I moved back to John's neck of the woods."

"You don't sound thrilled about the move."

"Supposed to be only for a few months, but I haven't landed anything except a few contract positions. I want to work at a research center. Monterey is top on my list. The coast is beautiful and the projects they're doing are cutting edge. Way more exciting than this."

Kara decided to poke a bit. "Free rent here, though, right?"

"That's been real generous of Ree. And she indulged me because I complained that we were crammed into the one-bedroom unit when a single guy was in the two-bedroom, and she convinced Vince to switch."

"That sounds like Ree."

Sonia shrugged. "I don't want to seem ungrateful, but in all honesty, we moved here because we had to. John left the university, and he was working for another hatchery farther south. We had a trailer that was at least close to town, and it was okay once we figured out the Wi-Fi, but the roof collapsed in that bad October storm. John looked Natalie up. He worked with Rocklin once upon a time, and Natalie put in a word with Ree. She hired John."

"John and Rocklin worked together? Where?"

"The same university in Washington. John was a professor and Rocklin was an executive of some sort. More acquaintances than friends, I guess, but John knew Rocklin and Natalie owned the stables, and their property was close to Ree's. One hatchery works as well as another for John."

"What do you think of Rocklin?" Kara said.

"Charming. He always complimented me."

"So you like him?"

"He has a temper, but so do I. I can understand why he left, to be honest. It's gotta be mind-numbing taking care of horses all day and night, though I think Natalie is way more hands-on about it. She loves them like pets, dotes on them, but he doesn't. Or didn't. John says he's in Europe, which sounds pretty good to me at this point. Maybe I'll look him up." Sonia's expression was coy.

*Maybe she already had.* Clearly, she admired Rocklin. Could she be working with him for some unknown reason?

Kara couldn't shake the feeling that he was involved in the trouble.

Sonia flipped a braid over her shoulder. "I probably shouldn't have shared all that. John's a great guy, but we just want different things. It's so…quiet here and too far away from the ocean. I'm a traveler, but John doesn't want to go any-where. I barely got him to go camping five miles from here. He won't even ride with me, even though Natalie says we can use her horses for free. Opposites attract, I guess." She frowned. "Ree's a bleeding heart, and I don't want to stay here taking advantage forever, but John watches the pennies, so he'll never leave unless I push." She looked out over the property and shivered. "During the day it's okay, but at night? All those acres of nothing? Wild things living and dying and hunting? That's just not for me. I want to have people around. Maybe Ree does too. Is that why she was thinking of selling?"

Kara's chin snapped up. "How did you know about that?"

Sonia waved a careless hand. "I overheard Natalie offering to buy a section of the property from Ree. She said no."

"Natalie?" Ree had never mentioned anything

about a discussion with Natalie. But Sonia was done with their chat.

"I promised John I'd sweep the amphitheater. Gotta dash."

Kara stared after her, stunned. What else didn't she know?

From the top of the ladder, Beau watched Kara and the dogs walking to join him. He enjoyed the easy way they moved together, as if they were a unit. For one intense moment, he craved to be part of that union, to be alongside Kara as she progressed through the world. What would it look like if he was there with her? It took him a second to realize it was the first time since the senior prom that he'd allowed himself to imagine being close to her. Maybe he should feel guilt or shame thinking of himself in Kyle's place, but instead he was caught up in the happiness of the image. Why would he dare to think about it now? Ludicrous, with a target on his back and his brain running a damaged program that made him out of sync with the world.

His musings were interrupted when a sheriff's squad car rolled up and an officer got out. Beau went through his mental checklist. Dark hair, mustache, the way the cop's left knee hitched. Sheriff Franco. Visiting now? His nerves fired, but he calmed himself.

If there had been a report about his mother, the hospital would have called him directly.

He climbed down from the ladder and brushed off the dust from his jeans.

Franco waved at Vince, Sonia and John, who were tending to various tasks in the picnic area.

"Hello, Beau. Kara," Franco said as he drew close. "Shaping up. Going to be ready for tomorrow?"

"Yes, sir." Beau accepted a bag Franco handed him with clothing inside. "Your mother's. We're done with them. Figured you'd want to bring her some clean ones when she's released."

With an effort, he swallowed the lump in his throat and thanked the sheriff.

Kara repeated what she'd learned about Natalie's offer to buy the property from Ree. Beau flat-out gaped. "And Mom didn't tell you about that? But you're the real estate agent."

Kara shook her head. "I'm new. Maybe she thought I didn't need to know because she'd declined it. Or maybe I just didn't ask her the right questions."

He didn't like her uncertainty, so he squeezed her shoulder. "Nothing to do with your competency, Kara. Didn't mean to imply that."

She lifted her chin again, and he felt the victory as her confidence returned. "I'm not sure it's relevant actually, but I didn't want to with-hold anything that might be helpful."

Franco hooked his thumbs in his belt loops. "I suppose if Natalie wanted to buy, and Ree didn't want to sell to her, that could be a motive, anger at her offer being refused, but it's not a convinc-ing one. Hurting or killing Ree still wouldn't ensure Natalie could buy the place. Might even decisively prohibit it because the whole sale is more complicated with the owner incapacitated. It also doesn't fit with the theory that this thing is connected to the November attack in any way that I can see."

Beau shook his head. "No, it doesn't."

Franco scratched his chin. "I took a look around the office area before I came here. You were right. No footprints discernable thanks to the pump failing or being tampered with. To be cautious, I'll have an officer posted on the prop-erty tonight, but she's finishing up in court. She'll be here by three. I've got to go back now, but I'll check in with you later. Oh. One more thing. My officers can't sort out any kind of evidence to show where Ree was initially attacked. We're going over the Security Hounds drone footage, and we'll let you know if anything pops."

Beau battled discouragement as he watched Franco leave. No evidence of what happened to his mom or where, or why she was moved. No indication who their paintball stalker or saboteur was. And nothing to tie the current trouble with his earlier attack. All of it meant the danger was still as potent as it had ever been.

Beau realized Kara was eyeing the bag of clothes in his hand until she shifted her attention to Millie, who had crept away to sprawl in a patch of sunlight. Phil appeared half asleep next to her. His stomach growled. "Hungry? My egg sandwich gave up on me hours ago. I'm starving."

"Me too."

"All right. My turn to fix the meal. Least I can do since you've been working like the proverbial dog all day."

Kara laughed and pointed to Millie and Phil piled together. "Like those sleepy pups?"

He chuckled. "We should have it so good. They had a rough night, like the rest of us."

Dogs retrieved, they departed, nodding to Vince, who was heaving a bag of charcoal to the barbecue pit. He slit it open with a pocket knife, sending the briquettes tumbling in.

Sonia and John sat in two folding chairs, their legs splayed out and crossed at the ankles. Sonia's head was propped on John's shoulder, and he'd tipped his hat down over his eyes. No one had gotten a good rest the night before, except for Sonia perhaps. Only an out-and-out flood had roused her to help that morning.

He waited while Kara gathered up the collapsible dog bowl, which needed a good washing now that Millie had shoved her paws in while she was drinking.

A woman with a saddle hustled by, an easel tucked under her arm. Natalie Clark, he told himself.

"We'll do rides every hour like we've always done," she told him as she pulled open the easel. "I'll write up the schedule. How's your mom?"

"Holding her own. Going to see her in a bit."

"Give her my love. I'll get started on more chicken soup."

Beau thanked her, picked up the clothes and joined Kara, who stood lost in thought, fingering her earring with the hand that wasn't holding the dog bowl.

"You know when you're thinking about something, you tug on your earring?"

She quickly let go of the small gold hoop. "What a tell. My brother Garrett bounces a tennis ball, and it drives us all bananas. I'll have to work on that."

"It's a subtle thing, better than a tennis ball. I've had to improve my observation skills." On impulse he gathered her to his side. "What's on your mind, Henny Penny?"

"Your mother's clothes." She pointed to the bag and lowered her voice. "If Millie can use them as a scent article and backtrack to where she was before she was dumped near the river, it might help us understand what happened."

He was already shaking his head before she finished. "I don't doubt Millie could follow the trail, and much as I'd love to try that..."

"You're concerned about an attack."

He nodded. "Reasonable to assume the troublemakers are still close. Best not to take any risks."

"We can do it safely. Have the sheriff Franco assigned come along for extra protection. She should be here while it's still daylight. We could go as soon as she arrives. That'd give us a couple of hours."

He kept hold of her shoulders as his thoughts ran ahead.

What if Millie could find the answer to what happened to his mom? Perhaps it would explain his own assault as well. Could it unmask the person or people who had stalked and attacked them both?

Should they take the risk? Should he allow her to do it?

As they walked back to the office with the dogs following, he felt like someone was staring at them, and he casually glanced behind him. Vince wiped his brow, apparently ignoring them from his spot by the grill.

John and Sonia were still sitting together, Sonia's head lying on John's shoulder. Beau thought she was asleep, but her eyes flicked open, staring at Beau intently before she closed them again. Sonia, the heavy sleeper.

Had she heard what Kara had proposed? Had John? Vince? Were they enemies or friends? It was the same problem he had to sort out with everyone he encountered since his injury. Who were they really? Just who they seemed to be? Or not?

The hours were rushing by, and this afternoon might be their one and only chance to follow Ree's trail and sniff out some answers.

He looked back at Vince, Sonia and John once more.

Would he find out the truth?

Or risk both their lives in the process?

# ELEVEN

They quickly ate the grilled cheese sandwiches Beau had prepared. The dogs wolfed their noon-time snack and Kara got them settled in the family room.

"I'd like to say they'll stay on the floor, but the moment we leave for the hospital, they'll both be up on the sofa before the door closes."

He laughed. "Fair. They deserve a little comfort too."

Dishes cleared, he was silently whipping up another round of arguments to dissuade Kara from her search idea as he escorted her to Big Blue for a quick hospital visit. She listened quietly, allowed him to say his piece, but did not change her decision. He was getting nowhere. Her family would surely try and put the kibosh on the idea. Perhaps he should call them, but in a way, it thrilled him, her quiet strength.

At the hospital, he snuck a quick look at his phone at the photo filed in the *People I Should*

*Know* folder. The first one was Ree. He'd added the caption *Your Mother*. Though it was truly humiliating to use a photo to remind him, he'd employ every tool available to help himself. It felt good to be proactive, planning instead of merely reacting or avoiding. He offered a silent thank you to God. In the midst of the storm, He was there, like He'd always been, that steady pulse of comfort. God would still recognize Beau...even in this new state of disarray he found himself.

And He'd restored Kara to Beau's world, returned the friend whom he needed more than he'd realized. Her chestnut ponytail swept her shoulder blades as she walked next to him, the sunlight catching her profile. His daydream took over. If this mess would only work out, then...

Then what? He'd stay and run the hatchery and have coffee with Kara every couple of months? That was suddenly not satisfying, not nearly enough.

They entered the hospital and took the elevator up to his mother's room. At the door, a uniformed security guard was squaring off with another man.

"What's the problem? You gotta frisk me or something?" the man growled.

The deep voice was easily recognizable.

"Vince," Kara mouthed, but Beau had already

arrived at that conclusion. Maybe he was improving.

"I just want to see her, is all," Vince said to the guard. "Want her to know I'm here. What's that gonna hurt with you watching from the doorway? What are you expecting me to do? Smother her with a pillow?"

"Sir, you're not on the list of family," the guard replied.

Vince pointed to Kara as they strode up. "Neither is she. Gonna let her in?"

"Sir…"

Vince appealed to Beau. "Come on, man. I've worked with your mom for over a decade, while you were away when there was no one else, before John and Sonia came on. It was just me and her and a whole bunch of work to be done." His chin went up and his mouth twisted. "Don't I have a right to see my friend? At least let her know that I haven't abandoned her?"

Like Beau had done to his mother after his injury? Running away when she was probably frantic about him? Vince wasn't going to beg, he was a proud man, but his tone indicated he was coming as close as possible to pleading. Beau didn't like to see any man humbled in such a way and neither would his mother. She trusted Vince. He spoke to the guard. "It's okay, while I'm here, just for a few minutes."

The security guard shrugged.

Vince let out a breath. "All right then."

Beau had a thought. "Vince, can I ask you something before you visit Mom?"

Vince shrugged. "Guess so."

"Were you aware my mother intended to sell the property?"

He jolted as if he'd been slapped. "Sell? Really? I never dreamed she would, though I sure suggested it a time or two. Too much for a woman her age. But…she didn't tell me anything about it." Hurt flashed across his face. Beau could relate to that feeling.

"Me neither."

"You didn't know?"

Beau shook his head. "She asked Kara to arrange the sale privately. Natalie knew, though, and she made an offer. Sonia overheard."

"Natalie?" His eyes narrowed. "How could she afford to buy it?"

"She only wanted a portion," Kara said.

"Hmm. Probably the Mesquite Trail access to compliment her stables." Vince paused. "You know her husband, Rocklin, made an offer for it years ago when your dad died."

Now it was Beau's turn to gape. Another tidbit he hadn't been aware of.

Kara appeared equally surprised.

Vince continued. "In poor taste, if you ask me,

and I told him as much. Pressing the advantage when she was grieving and all that."

Beau processed that startling fact. "Rocklin wanted the hatchery?"

"Purely for the earning potential. He was looking to purchase a profitable business. Natalie's passion for horses wasn't netting them much. He didn't care two bits for the fishery itself. Your mom and pop put in their blood, sweat and tears, and he wanted to take over the books and leave the running of it to others. That was his way. Lazy and greedy."

"Any idea how Sonia knew?"

"She's a busybody. Listens in on phone calls and pokes through the mail before it's opened. She doesn't belong here. Just grabbing the free rent, which I told Ree was way too generous. She should have cut that off after a month."

Beau blew out a breath. Sonia and John. Natalie and Rocklin. "This thing just keeps growing more heads."

"And it's not gonna go away." Vince stared at him. "You're a military man. Clearly there's an enemy around. Somebody clocked you over the head at Thanksgiving, right?"

Beau's eyes narrowed. "What do you know about that night?"

He shrugged. "Nothing much. I only went out looking for you when your mom came to me worried that you hadn't returned from your walk. Cops were already there by that time because you'd phoned them, but the call dropped off when you got clobbered. Made me wonder though."

"Wonder what?"

"If maybe you brought some enemies with you when you came home. And maybe that's what you're doing again now."

"I didn't bring any trouble with me, Vince. It was already here."

Vince shoved up the sleeves of his flannel shirt. His forearms were all wiry muscle. The skin on his cheeks was ruddy and windburned. He shook his head. "I didn't want her developing that trail in the first place. Made myself clear. Bad idea all around."

"Why? It would enhance the business, make it more attractive to a buyer, perhaps," Kara said.

"It'll be expensive, and she'll be trekking up there every free moment, supervising the workers. Bringing 'em lemonade and cookies. Photographing the whole thing for those nutty slideshows Sonia helps her put together."

"Mom's a savvy businesswoman, Vince. You know that. She believes the investment will pay off."

"That's not the point."

It irked him to be schooled by this man, who

felt he knew Ree better than Beau did. "What is the point?"

"Wake up, kid."

He bristled. "I'm not a kid, Vince. Say your piece."

"I dunno why I have to paint a picture for you." Vince's cheeks puffed as he blew out a breath. "Beau, your mom's heading toward seventy years old. How much longer you figure she can slave away at this place? Messed up her back good while you were deployed. Had to stay in bed for a solid two weeks. Didn't tell you that, huh? Barely kept the hatchery open. And then she caught pneumonia, and I almost didn't get her to the doctor in time for the meds. He said a few days longer and she'd have been in the emergency room."

Beau stared. He hadn't known any of it. So wrapped up in his own life. "She needs more help. I'm…"

"She's got more. John's here now, but he doesn't work any harder than he needs to. Sonia either. If someone, Rocklin or Natalie or whoever, wants to buy this place, I say let 'em. If it would get your mother to relax, then they're welcome to it." His face darkened. "Buyer would probably turn around and sell it again though. No one would love it like your mother."

"And you?"

Vince's mouth tightened. "I don't love this land, Beau, not like she does. It's her heart and soul."

Kara looked at Vince, chin cocked. "You really care about her."

Vince's face blanched. He looked at his boots, shoved up his sleeves again and straightened, still not quite meeting Beau's eyes. "We've been together a long time, me and your mom. Since right before your dad passed. I came to live here a few months prior to the funeral, and we've been working together since. Doesn't mean I can't try my best to take care of her, does it? You certainly haven't been around to do it."

Beau's flare of anger quickly died away. He'd been busy ferrying Marines from ship to shore all over the world, deployed to train Afghan army soldiers, helped with medivacs, provided heavy weapons fire support and maintained his armored vehicle down to the tiniest nut and bolt. Somehow, through all that, he'd never imagined his mom aging, slowing, struggling. Or maybe he'd never allowed himself to. Now he could hardly picture her at all. "I'm here now and I'm staying."

"What does that mean? Gonna take over the hatchery if she doesn't sell it?"

"I don't know."

"You'd better figure it out, because whether she's selling the place or not, your mom's got a right to know who she can count on and who she can't. Soon as she's got the doc's okay, she'll be on her feet again trying to do it all. And whoever's been causing trouble around here isn't gonna stop."

Beau looked at Vince closely. Might Vince have been behind the sabotage as a way to convince Ree to give up the hatchery? What was the emotion threading his words? Blame? A challenge? Protectiveness? Was Vince trying to cover up for his own involvement? Maybe he had been one of the men arguing when Beau was struck down, and he'd hurried back to his cabin, pretending to have been there all along.

Beau realized he had no idea whom to believe except for the gentle woman standing at his elbow. Kara, he would trust with his own life and his mother's.

"Okay if I talk to her now?" Vince snapped. "Before they tell me visiting hours are up?"

"Go ahead," Beau said.

Kara and Beau stepped into the hallway where they could watch, chatting quietly so as not to add to the awkwardness. The security guard kept an eye from the doorway.

Vince stood at the bedside, hands in his jeans pockets, mumbling softly to Ree, then waiting as if he were leaving space for her to answer. Her eyes remained closed. After a few moments, he hung his head and touched her arm.

As Vince shuffled out of the room, he darted a glance at Beau. "Thanks. I…uh, appreciate you letting me go in."

Beau nodded and Vince ambled away.

They took Vince's place at his mother's beside. Beau stroked one of her cheeks and Kara patted the other.

"Don't worry, Mom. We've got Pioneer Day under control." He wanted to tell her he was sorry he'd been so wrapped up in his own situation he hadn't thought about hers. He wanted to say that whoever had dumped her near the river had been caught and things would be shipshape when she returned. As he stared at every detail of her face, he knew his deepest craving was that when he next saw her, he would immediately know who she was.

He cleared his throat. "I sure would love to chat, Mom." Chat about why she wanted to sell and hadn't mentioned a word of it to him or Vince. "Can you wake up? Please?"

But her eyes remained closed, locked in with her own thoughts and dreams.

He kissed her cheek. "I love you. And I'm going to make everything work out." And if that meant starting over again without the hatchery, he'd do it. If he had to take a photo of every single person in Pine Bluff and carry it around with him, he'd do that too. Whatever was best for her. *Please let her recover, Lord. I need my mother.*

The doctor came to offer a report that Ree's vitals were strong, her blood pressure holding. "It's a waiting game," he said to end their conversation.

It felt like his whole existence was a waiting game.

He and Kara prayed over his mom, fingers clasped, and it calmed his heart and soul. After the amen, he was loath to let Kara go. This connection, whatever it was he felt for her, was growing stronger by the minute. The clamor of all the things that needed doing back at the hatchery pricked him as the afternoon hours began to wane.

They walked back to Big Blue and he kept his head on a swivel. It would be a strange place for someone to stage an attack, but strange was becoming the new normal. He felt Kara tug at his sleeve.

"You're going too fast."

"Sorry." He matched his stride to hers. "Trying to figure out Vince's involvement in all this."

She arched a brow at him. "Don't you see?"

"See what?"

"Vince's connection to your mother."

"Yes, they've been friends a long time. I…"

"Not friendship, Beau. It's completely obvious."

"What is?"

"Vince is in love with her."

\* \* \*

Kara was still amazed as they returned to the hatchery that Beau hadn't realized what was so obvious. Vince was in love with Ree. It was clear in his gentleness toward her, the grief in his tone when he whispered at her bedside.

It didn't mean that Vince couldn't have done something terrible, she reminded herself, and he could very well still be part of the plot against Beau, but at least that much was now clear. When they returned to the hatchery, the office phone was ringing. Beau hurried to get it.

Millie and Phil hustled over to her, snuffling up wafts of her scent as if she were wearing exotic perfume. "Easy," she said, avoiding Millie's drool. "I know you've been cooped up too long." They were capable of power-napping, but they'd clearly decided the rest period was over. She rescued a lamp from being overturned by Millie's powerfully whipping tail.

Finished with their examination, the dogs rushed to the sliding door, eager to be let out into the small, fenced yard where Ree kept a tiny propane barbecue and a table and chairs beside the scraggly lawn. "All right, dogs. Hold your horses."

She slid the door open, and the dogs charged out. Kara followed. The yard was shadowed by the tall wooden fence. Immediately she felt that something was off. The dogs raced to the far corner of the yard, where a paper plate lay on the ground. She tried to see around them. It wasn't simply windblown trash, something was weighing it down. Her stomach clenched.

She shouted as they raced toward the plate, but they didn't even register her command in their excitement. Whatever it was, she could not let them get to it until she'd checked it carefully, but they were bulldozing forward, noses twitching. "Leave it!" she yelled, her panic rising as the dogs skidded to a stop almost on top of the foreign object. She started toward them, yelling for Beau. As she leapt from the last step, a noise immediately to her left in the shadows near the gate caught her attention. She jerked toward the sound, arm raised instinctively. Something heavy and metallic arced near her face. She ducked, losing her footing and falling to a knee just as someone slammed a shovel where her head had been. Chips of stucco peppered her face.

She landed on her hands and knees in the soggy grass, rolling to the side, away from the attacker. The dogs about-faced and galloped at her, barking at full volume. She saw a shovel launched through the air, straight at Millie.

# TWELVE

"Millie!" Kara screamed.

Phil leapt in front of the bloodhound and batted the wooden handle with his front paws, causing it to veer away, falling harmlessly to the grass. Kara got to one knee as she heard whoever it was shove through the gate and disappear. Beau erupted from the house, hurtling down the steps to her side.

"I'm okay," she said pointing. "There's something in the yard. Gotta keep it away from the dogs."

The dogs' attention was on her, so Beau jogged to the corner and snatched up the paper plate.

Millie was still poking her nose at Kara's face in concern as she got to her feet on shaky legs, brushing the dirt off her jeans. "Hold," she told Millie as she hurried to peer through the open gate, but all she saw was the grassy field and the amphitheater in the distance. Quickly she ducked back in the house and grabbed a pair of binoculars. Frustration bit at her as she scanned. No one was visible at all so she wasn't even able to rule out any of the employees as the possible attacker.

She kicked the gate closed and turned to Beau.

He was hustling back to her, holding the plate to examine it.

Two greasy hot dogs were speckled in some sort of powder. Her skin went hot and then cold as she met Beau's eyes. "Someone was trying to poison my dogs, or at least drug them."

"So we wouldn't carry out our search," Beau said grimly as he looked at the gouge where the shovel had hit.

If it had been her skull…fear and fury hummed in her nerves. Her innocent dogs, her babies had been made targets. This must be how parents felt when there was a threat to their child. It was visceral, personal.

"Inside," Beau said.

She didn't argue. The dogs were still confused as they returned, quivering and jumpy. Beau scooted the paper plate far back on the kitchen counter. "Would they have eaten the food?"

"I'm not positive. They're taught not to take anything unless they have permission, but they're dogs, after all. Roman's dog Wally's food thievery is legendary." She tried to keep her tone light, but she was still shaking. "I'm scared and outraged and disgusted all at once." Tears flooded her eyes and she blinked them away. "Someone could have killed my dogs."

"Or you." He escorted her to a chair and knelt next to her. "Tell me again that you're not hurt, Henny Penny."

His blue irises reflected her face back at her as he gently stroked her cheek. The warmth seeped through the pounding staccato of her nerves. "Yes, I'm okay, but if I hadn't ducked…"

The shovel blow could have fractured her skull…or worse.

He pressed his forehead to hers. "Imagining what could have happened will be a thought that keeps me up at night." He sighed. "You shouldn't be here, Kara. It's dangerous and you're too precious to be put at risk."

*Precious.*

He pulled back to look at her again and kissed her. It was a light touch on the lips, and it sparked an unexpected longing inside her, opening up a place that had been empty since Kyle passed away. Then Beau kissed her again and she returned it. So sweet and warm and perfect. *Precious.* It ended too soon when he moved back and shook his head, standing and turning away from her.

"I shouldn't have done that."

She cocked her head at him. "Why not?" It felt as natural and right as could be.

"It's… I told myself I never would…try and get close, once Kyle fell in love with you."

"Kyle's gone, Beau," she said softly. "And he only wanted the best for the people he loved. You and me."

He blanched and fiddled with his pocket. "I know. Sometimes it feels like he's still here."

She shook her head and it was as if all the bottled up words had been jarred loose by what had almost happened in the yard. "Watching Kyle die, I felt completely powerless. I couldn't cure him or ease his suffering. At the end I wasn't even able to make him smile, he was hurting so much. I didn't think I could cope, continue sitting at his bedside day after day, watching his mother mourn, his sister trying her best to cry silently so Kyle wouldn't hear her. I thought I'd break. It was too much." Her voice wobbled.

Beau dropped his gaze to the floor as if it were too much for him to think about too.

She folded her hands in her lap and took a breath. "But God showed me that I could stand up to it, not just for Kyle but for myself. I had a reservoir of strength I'd not realized because I'd never had to tap into it. When I did, God added His strength to my pittance, and it was enough. I was enough. Kyle passed into the next life knowing how much he was loved in this one."

Beau's voice came out a murmur. "Yes, he knew. He sure did."

"So, now I know I'm strong and He loves me, and being able to stand with Kyle through it all was a gift to both of us. It came with a lot of pain, no question, but I learned I can tell the truth, even when it's scary." She stood up and faced him. "I'll be clear, Beau, because I know how short life can be. I care about you. I've always cared about you, even when I was in love with Kyle, because my heart is big enough to have love and friendship together. But we're more than friends now. I know you feel it too."

His expression was puzzled. Hopeful? It flashed on her how extremely difficult the inability to read faces would be. She couldn't decipher his emotions, so she plunged on. "After what we've been through, I hope you can see me for who I am, not just Kyle's bereaved fiancée. He was an amazing man, and I'll always love him and so will you. Can't we allow that to bond us closer instead of standing between us?"

He huffed out a breath. "You've changed, Kara, and so have I, but now…" He spread his hands as if he were letting something go. "I can't recognize you or anyone. How can—"

A sharp rap on the door sent the dogs scrambling into motion, hurtling onto the sofa to look out the front window.

Kara winced. Had the interruption saved her from a humiliating rejection? Or stopped them from finally getting past the obstacle of Beau's condition? There was nothing to do but wait and command the dogs into a sit as Beau opened the door for a uniformed sheriff.

The woman's short bob of blond hair was pinned neatly behind her ears. "Sheriff Talia Carpenter."

They made the introductions and Carpenter listened attentively while Beau and Kara explained what had happened in the yard. The sheriff took a look while they waited.

"Photographed the shovel. I'll bag it and transport for analysis along with the hot dogs. No tracks that I can see. Woman or man, do you think?"

Kara closed her eyes and tried to replay the situation. "It could have been a woman or a slender man."

"Got both around here," Beau said. "Had to have been someone on the property, so we're back to John, Sonia, Vince…"

"And Natalie was here today too, setting up her riding schedule on the whiteboard," Kara reminded him.

"But none of them were close enough to overhear our search plans, were they?"

The sheriff bagged the plate of hot dogs. "One

of them was, and that's all it would take to spread the news."

"Spread the…" She finally understood what the sheriff was insinuating. "You're suggesting it could be more than one of them involved."

"Or all three." She finished typing notes into her cell phone. "You still want to go through with this search?"

Did she?

She felt Beau watching her. He would not insist. As a matter of fact, he'd argue again to forget the whole plan.

Her gut told her the answers lay buried out there in a place only Millie could find.

Was she willing to risk it for Ree? For Beau?

Slowly, she nodded. "It's the only way."

Beau's nerves prickled like barbed wire. The potential consequences of the mission were more than he could swallow. His only consolation was that they had a sheriff along, and Kara's family would arrive in a matter of hours from what she'd told him. They'd strenuously requested the search be delayed, Chase sending him so many texts to that effect he finally put his phone on vibrate mode. But Kara was right, in that a nighttime search would be even riskier, so the window was closing.

At half past three, he'd stripped his gun, cleaned

and reassembled it, packed his gear and waited, while Kara leashed Millie under Phil's supervision. As they headed with the sheriff to the trail, he wondered who might be watching.

The sheriff took a position at his shoulder, with Kara holding Millie's leash and Phil in tandem. He was pleased to see Carpenter was as alert as he was, constantly scanning. She was in excellent condition, tackling the slope around the slide to the overlook and down into the meadow that led to the river where he'd taken an unexpected swim with Phil. The log bridge was still knocked loose, another thing he'd need to tend to at some point. Kara pulled out the bag with his mother's clothes and let Millie take a whiff.

The bloodhound trotted down to the water. Phil whined.

"Steady on, Phil," he said. "No diving in this time." He figured they'd have to hike the two miles or so downstream and wade across where the river shallowed out. As if in confirmation, Millie headed to a narrow ribbon of a path and forced them to go single file near the gurgling water. Why would his mother have gone this way? It led to the Mesquite Trail. He'd enjoyed it with his father often as a boy, particularly when his father brought the ropes along for…

"The caves," he blurted.

Carpenter slowed. "What?"

"There are caves beyond the turnoff to the Mesquite. They flood during the spring season. In the past, years ago, we had some people trespassing. Curiosity seekers, mostly, young people who snuck in on foot and decided to do some exploring. My dad had to threaten them with the police because they came back. What if Mom saw some trespassers? Went to confront them?"

Carpenter considered. "Plausible, but if they were responsible for the attack, why move her body?"

"I don't know." But it somehow felt as if the answers had to be in those caves.

Clearly Millie was leading them in that direction, because she'd pulled the long leash taut in her excitement. They half jogged, half walked for a quarter mile until they came to a place where the trail turned a corner and provided a view of a rocky gorge dipping away from their position.

Millie turned in excited circles and sat with droopy jowls quivering, staring at Kara.

"Here," Kara said. "Ree must have been here when she was knocked out."

He stood in the spot Millie indicated, turning in all directions. Behind them, in the distance, the overlook shone in the waning sunlight. A ninety-degree turn put him in a position to look down at the rugged tumble of boulders and the weather-worn cliffs that hid the caves.

What if she'd seen something? Someone with a flashlight? She'd been knocked out from behind, similar to what had happened to him. There were plenty of rocks and trees where an attacker could have hidden to launch their assault. His gaze wandered up along the trail, where it would join up to the main one, where he himself had been struck down. He considered. Probably three miles from the place he'd been discovered to this spot, as the crow flew. The threads of connection still eluded him, yet his instincts twitched. The two situations were tied together. He didn't know how, but he was dead certain he was getting closer.

Millie and Phil gulped their reward while the sheriff photographed the ground Millie alerted on. There was no outward sign of a weapon, no rock or branch that might have been used to bludgeon her, but that could easily have been tossed away by whoever had moved her.

"Another hour and we call it quits," Carpenter said. "Caves?"

"Caves," he confirmed. "I can point us to a couple of them that might be accessible now that the water's begun to recede. The lower passages will still be submerged."

"We're not doing any spelunking," Carpenter said sharply. "This is strictly recon and report. Got me?"

Both he and Kara nodded, and he moved closer to Kara's side.

"My brothers can get us some drone imaging tomorrow before Pioneer Day kicks off. Maybe even tonight if they get here quick enough."

Pioneer Day felt like a relic from someone else's past. The thought of crowds coming for entertainment while they searched for answers to a violent attack was too much to assimilate. They climbed down a twisting route until they came to a protruding shelf of rock that provided a view of the panorama. He pointed to the dark triangular gap below them. "That's one of the caves, the largest. There's another fifty yards to the right."

"I see it."

He pulled his binoculars out again and focused on the mouth of the cave. "What's that?"

"What?" Kara peered through her own binoculars.

"That gray thing."

"Looks like a piece of rubber," Kara said, but Beau was already climbing down, ignoring Carpenter's remark that he should stay put and let her do it.

His mother. His problem. His life.

And Kara's. The sooner he could get her back to the office, the better, and he was more familiar with the terrain than Carpenter was. Plus, he knew that Carpenter would not leave Kara alone.

"Only be a minute," he called up. He hadn't explored the caves since he was a kid. The rock clusters were unfamiliar, and some had slid loose or collapsed. Natural weathering? Animals? Someone trying to hide the access so others wouldn't find an entrance? He made his way to the mouth of the larger cave and the item that had caught his attention.

He used his fingertips to snag the five-inch piece of a tarp that had gotten trapped between two rocks. Litter, likely, blown in by the capricious wind. Disappointment stabbed at him. Nonetheless, he shoved it into his pocket.

"Let's go, Mr. O'Connor," Carpenter called. "We're almost out of daylight." It was clear from the sheriff's tone she wasn't going to brook any arguments. They were in agreement anyway. Dusk would bring its own dangers. They had a starting point for the police to conduct a more thorough search, and he'd be right there to assist…as soon as Kara was delivered safely home.

"Copy that," he called. As he ascended and rejoined them, he heard a bullet explode the granite inches from his head.

Kara screamed.

Beau reached for Kara, but she and Sheriff Carpenter had dropped to the ground. He did the same. Kara shielded the dogs, an arm around Millie as Phil barked.

"Beau?" Kara's voice quavered.

"I'm okay. You two?"

"Not hurt."

"Me neither," Carpenter said.

That was one prayer answered. Another rifle shot bit into the tree next to them.

Carpenter pulled her weapon and fired, the noise sending the dogs into a barking frenzy. He readied his gun also, but he was uncertain where to aim. The pines to their right? The pillar of rock that sloughed off into crumbling cascades of debris? He needed to be wary of a ricochet.

There was another shot, then one more from their enemy, and then the gun fell silent. Carpenter, breathing hard, called for backup.

Beau belly-crawled to Kara's other side, snuggling next to the two furry bodies. "Dogs okay too?"

She nodded, eyes wide as silver dollars.

"Think the shooter's gone?" he asked Carpenter.

"Likely. Backup's en route, but we're not moving until I'm sure it's safe."

Kara's phone buzzed, and with shaking hands, she answered. Beau could clearly hear every syllable from her agitated brother.

"We're on scene," Chase snapped. "I heard shots. Where are you?"

Beau was relieved to know the Wolfes were close.

Kara reported what had happened.

"Garrett's getting the drone up and I'm on the way."

"Negative," Carpenter called out. "We'll wait for police backup. Do not move to our location."

But there was no reply. Chase hadn't heard or had chosen to ignore the directive.

"Sorry, Sheriff Carpenter," Kara said apologetically. "He's coming."

Forty minutes later, Chase texted: Arriving in two. No sign of shooter.

They stood slowly, Beau in front of Kara. The dogs were maintaining a sit, but they both perked up when Chase and Tank appeared.

"Chase Wolfe," her brother called out, palms upraised for the officer's benefit.

They exchanged a quick back-and-forth and Chase hustled to his sister. "We're moving out of here. Now."

But before they could, hoofbeats echoed across the grass. He, Chase and Sheriff Carpenter palmed their weapons as Natalie rode into view. She pulled the horse to a hard stop with one hand and held up the other.

"Don't shoot. I'm the neighbor. I came to help."

Carpenter drew closer, and Chase and Beau covered her until they were all certain Natalie Clark was unarmed as she slid off her horse, hands still raised.

They lowered their weapons.

"Why are you here, Ms. Clark?" Carpenter asked.

"I heard a shot. I tried to call Vince and John, but they didn't answer. I worried it was a mountain lion or something."

"No. A random shooter."

Her brows shot up. "Shooting at what?"

"Ms. Clark, ride back to the office now, please," Carpenter commanded. "We'll talk it all out there."

Natalie nodded, hopped easily back into the saddle and rode off. They followed, Chase and Beau taking up positions on either side of Kara and the dogs. His pulse still raced as they hurried along the trail in the rising gloom.

This time it was not paint pellets being fired in their direction.

Bullets.

Meant to kill?

He moved closer to Kara as they progressed. They couldn't cover the ground fast enough for his taste.

Natalie was waiting at the office when they arrived shortly before a police car tore up the drive.

The sheriff with the mustache got out, Franco. Sheriff Franco and Carpenter assembled everyone inside.

Kara's other brother joined them, obviously frustrated as he laid his drone on the table. "I got nothing. Heavy tree coverage and no movement that the camera could detect." He clasped her in a bear hug, and Beau felt a tug of envy that he wasn't the one doing the comforting.

The officers took each person's initial statement before he started in on a second round of follow-up questions. Franco began a conversation with Garrett, Chase and Carpenter.

Beau followed Kara as she led the dogs to the kitchen, where she offered water and treats. The near miss stoked a fire in his nerves, and he thanked God she and her faithful dogs hadn't been hurt, or Carpenter or her brothers.

Kara took mugs from the cupboard and measured out coffee. He could easily have done it himself, but he saw her fingers shaking and understood she needed a task.

Natalie, arms folded, joined them. "I don't understand what's happening."

"You and me both, Natalie," he said.

"Why would a shooter come here? What's in it for them?"

Kara offered her a cup of coffee. "I don't know. What do you think?"

She huffed out a breath, eyes widening. "I can't even begin to imagine. There's not much worth stealing here. And Ree leads a quiet life. Who would want to hurt her? Or you, Beau?" She waved a vague hand. "Or anyone else around here."

"Have you ever had any problems like this before?" Kara said.

"No, not as long as I've owned the stables." She shivered. "Maybe I should have been more alert. I love being out here, but it's not the city, where you can call out and someone will hear you. Of course, Rocklin would remind me that people in the city wouldn't come running even if they did hear a shout for help." She sniffed.

"I heard that you offered to buy some of my mom's land."

Natalie blinked. "You did? I thought Ree would keep that private."

"She did. I heard it from someone else."

"Who?"

When Beau didn't answer, Natalie rolled her eyes. "Never mind. I did offer. Sonia told me she'd heard Ree on the phone speaking about listing the property, and it got me to thinking. I'm not keen on someone buying it up who might develop the land or something. I knew money was tight for Ree, and I figured it would enhance the stables to own the property around the riding trail. My ex-husband tried to buy the whole thing decades ago too, as a matter of fact. He was the kind of guy who would pressure a woman who'd just lost her husband for his own personal gain." Again she looked at Beau. "You know what type of man he was."

He did. Not one he ever wanted to meet again. Franco was still talking to Chase and Garrett and taking copious notes. Carpenter left, and Beau watched her knock on both Vince's and the Partridges' front doors. No response at Vince's. Sonia answered, holding a water bottle. Was John with her?

He wondered where Vince had gotten to. There were plenty of legitimate reasons why he wasn't at home.

Beau offered Kara a smile of encouragement, but his attention flicked back to Natalie, who declined Kara's offer of coffee. Both Natalie and Rocklin had wanted Ree's property for one reason or another. And his mom had granted neither's request.

Motive? But Natalie hadn't had a rifle on her person when she'd arrived at the scene of the shooting and another officer had combed the area and not found one discarded. Did that mean Natalie wasn't an enemy? Not completely. She could have dumped the weapon somewhere. But as she herself pointed out, what was the purpose of it all? He eyed the fragment of tarp in a plastic bag on the kitchen table. A random scrap? A clue? A headache burgeoned behind temples. At the core he was a Marine, not a detective. He prayed Chase and Garrett would have some insight. He realized he'd missed Natalie's last remark.

"Then again, a guy who would take off and leave a child he'd raised since she was a baby has a character problem." Natalie noted Kara's inquisitive look. "My daughter Fallon's father and I divorced before she was even born. Rocklin and I met when she was almost two. She doesn't know any other father. Sure he sends birthday cards and texts, but it's always accompanied by an excuse about why he can't visit her. Too far, too busy, too expensive—the tightwad."

Beau could not imagine how that would feel for a child, no matter what their age, to have a father pay no attention.

Natalie shrugged. "At least now he can't savage me for spending money on horses. Not his business anymore, is it?" She brightened. "I've got a new foal coming in May, and Fallon is as excited about it as I am. Ree too. She suggested we name it after Fallon." Natalie lifted her chin and her mouth wobbled.

A boulder formed in Beau's throat. "Mom's going to be well enough to welcome that foal. I'm certain of it."

"She's been my one true friend through the whole Rocklin debacle. She doesn't deserve what she's gotten." Pain shimmered on her face. "Do you think the police will tell us to cancel Pioneer Day?"

That would likely be a financial blow to Natalie as well as the hatchery. "Until we hear otherwise, it's full speed ahead."

Natalie grinned. "Now you sound like your mom."

The compliment buoyed him. If they could get through Pioneer Day and the police could analyze the spot Millie had pointed out where Ree was struck down, maybe they would be able to put the whole terrible matter to rest.

He darted a look at Kara. And then…he'd start living again…somehow. He watched Kara murmur quietly to Millie and Phil, who stared at her adoringly.

Garrett and Chase made plans to stay, their mother promising to join when the details from their last mission were concluded. They'd not had time to bring the RV, so Beau did the best he could with the sleeping arrangements after he checked last-minute Pioneer Day details. He saw no sign of John or Vince.

Dinner was a quiet affair of pizza Garrett picked up in town. Kara's brothers prepared to spend the night on the office sofa and love seat,

Chase's long legs sticking up over the armrest. Their dogs piled together, while Kara and hers returned to their upstairs room.

He knew the Wolfes didn't want their sister involved.

He didn't either, not in the danger part, but he couldn't deny that his spirit felt better, lighter, more hopeful with Kara close by. How would Kyle feel about that? The thought pricked a hole in his optimism.

The mission ahead was clear. Handle the chaos the next day would bring while making sure Kara and the dogs stayed safe.

*Pioneer Day, here we come.*

# THIRTEEN

Kara woke long before her alarm the next morning. She'd listened to a church service online that Beau told her about, since they could not make it into town.

Both she and Beau were fueled up with coffee well in advance of the first wave of visitors, which started as a trickle after sunup and turned into a gush. Garrett and Chase patrolled the grounds with their dogs, who garnered lots of attention from the visitors. The saggy, baggy bloodhounds were always up for a meet-and-greet and a swift lick of a child's sticky hand. It was all so festive, and she could hardly reconcile the beautiful event with the fear she'd felt the night before as someone shot at them.

Phil and Millie stayed close and got their own share of attention, though Phil kept his distance. The kids came and went, a continual stream of them occupying her picnic table. As she finished her midmorning craft session, she was surprised to see a man she recognized, Hal Green, the broker she'd dealt with regarding the hatchery sale. *What's he doing here?* She'd told him the sale was on pause due to Ree's injury.

He greeted her with a chin bob. "Thought I'd come check it out, in spite of you tapping the brakes. Got a potential client for you, but he has some reservations. Figures maybe the asking price will drop if the listing lingers, and really, how many people are in the market for a fish hatchery?"

She gave a noncommittal shrug. "Time will tell."

"Any other offers?"

She smiled. "You know I'm not able to share that with you, Hal."

He grinned back. "Never hurts to ask, right?" She watched him slide on a pair of sunglasses and step away as his phone buzzed. He spoke and the name jumped out at her.

"Hello, Rocklin," Hal said.

*Rocklin?*

"I think they're bluffing," Hal continued. "Don't think they have any other interest. With the owner being laid up, the whole thing might be on hold for a bit, but I can put in your offer and…" He gripped the phone. "Why? There's no reason not to take a shot at it and see…" He broke off. "All right. Fine. You call me when you want to pick it up again."

Hal shoved the phone in his pants pocket and strode away.

Rocklin was still in the picture?

Distracted, Kara clumsily tipped the plate of finger paint over, and it splattered her shirt. The liquid soaked through to her skin. Great. "Come on, dogs. I have to go change."

With people enjoying the music, plenty of visitors and Millie and Beau at her side, she felt perfectly safe hustling back to the office to grab a clean shirt. *Rocklin*, she mused as she waved to Sonia, Vince and her brothers. What did his involvement mean?

She dodged a family pulling a wagon full of toddlers, and she jogged to the office.

Phil spun and looked behind them with a growl.

Breath caught, she followed his gaze but saw only a stream of people walking along the raceways, others queuing up for the barbecue lunch. The whole situation was making her paranoid. She quickened her pace. Beau had locked the doors and given her the key, so she let herself in and quickly found a clean T-shirt.

The dogs slopped up water in the kitchen as she prepared to leave again. She noticed the bag on the counter with the piece of tarp inside.

Franco must have forgotten to take it. She peered through the plastic, her gaze snagging on a tiny shred of color. She took out her phone, snapped a picture and enlarged it.

A miniscule bit of material or maybe a snip of yarn. Yellow. Why did the color strike a familiar chord?

She bent closer, distracted by a scrabble of paws on the floor. In a flash, Millie scooted over, reared up on her back legs and snatched the plastic bag from the counter. Kara was so startled she couldn't get out a command before Millie slammed her way out the front door, which Kara hadn't locked, the bag clenched in her teeth.

Phil looked every bit as startled, but his reaction time was faster, and he galloped after his charge. Kara shook off her shock and sprinted in pursuit, yelling. Millie didn't slow. She raced across the office property, beelining between the residences as Phil bumped and smacked her away from the walls of the structures.

"Millie!" she shouted, squelching through muddy patches as she chased the dog. They emerged to the rear of Vince's house, and Millie butted the door of a shed with her bony skull. Surprisingly, it flew open, and she disappeared inside with a swish of her tail, ignoring both Kara's commands and Phil's annoyed bark.

"This means a retraining class, you stinker,"

Kara called as she hurried into the shed. She'd grab the dogs and get out, hopefully before anyone noticed the canine trespassing. How she'd explain the evidence theft to Franco was another matter.

"Millie," she snapped, her eyes adjusting to the dark to find the bloodhound with her nose glued to a stack of tarps, ears flapping in triumph, the baggie with the bit of torn fabric dangling from her saggy lips. Her message was clear. This was the tarp from which the torn piece at the caves had originated.

A cold chill swept over Kara as she looked at the neatly folded tarps. So Vince had moved the one with the fragment of yellow thread from his garage to the caves and then returned it to rest innocuously among the others. Why? What would he need a tarp for?

Yellow.

Again the word circled in her mind again until it clicked.

In Beau's phone call to the police the night he'd been struck down, he'd said he thought one of the men arguing had been wearing yellow.

*Get out.* Goose bumps erupted all over her body as she summoned the dogs. They turned, just as the side shed door was pulled shut. She tugged, but it would not open. With a surge of panic, she pushed at it, kicked and shoved, but it remained locked or jammed.

Her screams echoed back at her.

With frantic fingers, she reached for her phone as she caught a familiar acrid smell.

Gasoline.

And then she heard the sizzle of a match.

She grabbed the dogs and hauled them with her to the far corner of the shed, ignoring the spiderwebs and garden tools that poked at her. Smoke slithered under the door and the crackle of flames was louder as the fire took hold of the weathered doorframe.

She fumbled with her phone to dial the first number that came up.

"Beau…" The smoke stung her eyes and nose, and she began to cough. Within seconds, the heat soared as the shed filled with toxic air.

"Kara, where are you? What's wrong?"

She tried to tell him, but she couldn't stop coughing. The dogs pushed against her legs, howling their confusion.

His voice rose in volume, the fear tangible. "Kara…"

With a pop, the fire devoured the entire wall. There was no way anyone could get through those flames…

"Shed…" she managed before she fell to her knees.

\* \* \*

Beau exploded into action as he clutched his phone and ran. "I'm coming. Hold on."

"What…?"

Beau didn't stop to answer Chase's question as he sprinted by. There were other shouts that faded into the background, all sank under the fear of what might be happening to Kara.

There were several sheds on the property, but the closest were the two behind the employee residences. He picked up the sharp scent of smoke.

Kara…

He ran past the office and through the narrow alley, noting the squishy dog footprints that would have directed him if the roiling smoke wasn't enough.

The shed was belching black smoke, orange flames hopping. Several people arrived on the scene, but he didn't take the time to sort them all out. "Fire extinguisher in the office kitchen," he shouted.

Garrett—or maybe it was John—ran off to fetch it.

He shouted her name. He might have heard a reply, but he couldn't tell over the sizzling of the old wood. He could see through the smoke that there was a metal wedge crammed in under the door, keeping it from opening. With a slam of his boot, he kicked it free. The door had collapsed a few inches, impeding the hinges, so he tried breaking through it with his body.

His left shoulder screamed in pain as the fabric of his shirt caught fire. A man—curly haired, brother? Chase?—stripped off his own jacket and batted out the flames.

"Together," Chase shouted and gave him a silent three-fingered countdown. Their combined body weight splintered the resistant door, twisting it free.

He plowed through, Chase right behind. The smoke made it nearly impossible to see, but he heard the dogs barking to his left. He hunched and felt his way over until he touched her shin, her knee. That was enough to orient himself, and he grabbed her around the waist, hoisted her over his shoulder and ran for the door. He thought the two dogs were following, but Chase would check.

A dark-haired guy with sharp blue eyes worked the extinguisher. Garrett. In a moment two women and a man raced up, carrying two more extinguishers between them. The women applied the foam while the man, John Partridge—he remembered from the goatee—spun the outside faucet and slung the garden hose over and began to douse the flames.

He ran with Kara in his arms until the worst

of the smoke was behind them before he knelt and put her on the ground, propped with her back against the side of Vince's house. Gut clenched, he reached for her, brushing the hair away from her closed eyes.

"Kara…" He could not force any words out as her lids fluttered open and she looked at him. Chase dropped to his knees, and suddenly the two dogs were there, whining and licking at Kara, who wrapped an arm around each of them.

Her face was streaked with soot and tears, and her breathing was fast in between coughing fits.

"The dogs…" she rasped to Chase.

"I'll check them over in a minute."

"Now," she said with surprising force.

Chase acquiesced and began to examine the dogs while Beau clung to Kara's hands. What had the smoke done to her lungs?

"Millie snatched the evidence back with the tarp in it," she gasped out.

The evidence bag? His stomach dropped. "You can tell me later."

After a cough, she shook her head vehemently. "She ran to the shed with it. The tarp was there and there was a yellow thread stuck on it. Yellow—" she coughed some more "—like the color of the sweater the person was wearing when you were attacked."

Her revelation was mind-boggling, but it didn't dampen his fear. "Henny Penny, we'll sort that all out. What matters now is that you and the dogs are okay."

Chase finished his cursory exam. "Dogs are filthy but unharmed. Garrett's going to take them straight to the vet hospital as a precaution. Medics are rolling for you. Carpenter is keeping the crowds back."

"The bag," Kara said, eyes wide in her smoke-stained face. "With the piece of tarp."

Beau allowed himself a look at the blazing shed.

Whatever evidence there had been that might tell a story was now obliterated.

Beau's jaw clenched. He'd get his answers, and he wasn't going to let Kara undergo one more moment of risk. He sat with her until the medics arrived. Sonia, John and Natalie returned to the activities to finish up the last few hours so he could drive to the hospital. As Garrett took the dogs and Kara was loaded onto a gurney with an oxygen mask over her face, he felt Chase's hand on his shoulder.

He turned. "You don't need to say it, Chase. Her involvement is over."

"We'll help you get answers however we can. You'll need to make it clear to Kara. She won't walk away from this unless you give her no other alternative." Chase clapped him on the back. "Sorry it had to come to this, man."

As Beau watched him hustle off, he was already working out what he'd say to Kara. He turned it over in his mind multiple times as he drove again to the hospital.

He understood he'd need to be clear that he wanted her to leave.

Though his heart was already screaming in protest.

*No choice, Beau.*

At the hospital, Sheriff Franco was already waiting with the rumpled Chase when he arrived. Kara's brother had black soot all over him and Beau realized he did too. And they both smelled like a charcoal briquette.

"Doctors are examining Kara now," Chase said. "I was giving Franco the rundown."

Beau nodded. "She called me, clearly in trouble. She only got one word out." And it still carved a terrifying path through his soul. If she hadn't managed a call…if he hadn't found her so quickly… Dry-mouthed, he listened to the sheriff.

"Someone was watching her, clearly. Saw the dog run out of the office with the plastic bag.

Took the opportunity to trap her in the shed and destroy the tarp evidence in one move."

"A tarp used for what?" Chase asked.

"Good question. We're looking for Vince Greyson to fill us in, since the attempted murder of Ms. Wolfe and her dogs went down in his backyard, but he doesn't seem to be on the property. My deputy said he'd told the others there was a last-minute delivery request he'd decided to fulfill since Pioneer Day was winding down."

Chase frowned. "Convenient."

"Yes. We'll check out his alibi."

Beau shared what Kara said about the yellow thread. "The guy I saw the night I was clobbered. I thought he was wearing something yellow."

Franco didn't exactly look convinced, but he dutifully wrote it down. "We'll get a team to check the caves as soon as we finish assisting the fire department with the arson investigation, but there's not a lot to go on here with a burned up tarp and the shed completely fried. Ms. Wolfe showed me a picture she took of the bag with the yellow thread, but it's not going to be much help without the evidence itself."

Franco excused himself, and he and Chase waited in morose silence, interrupted only by Chase stepping away and quietly explaining the situation to his mother and other siblings. After another half hour, Chase reported on a text he'd just received.

"Garrett says the dogs are okay. He's getting them cleaned up and bringing them here because Kara will insist on seeing them."

That she would.

And she'd put up a fuss when he sent her away too, but it couldn't be helped.

They jumped to their feet when the doctor came to report that Kara suffered only mild smoke inhalation and was cleared to be released.

Beau almost shouted his hallelujah aloud.

Chase went in to see her first, emerging after a short while, brusque and determined. "I'll drive her to the hatchery so we can get our gear and her car."

And to be certain Kara was leaving the hatchery grounds.

The thought of facing the next day without her, and the one after that and the parade of days that might pass by before her attacker was caught, felt like a physical blow.

"She's asking for you." Chase's voice held a warning.

"I'll make sure she's prepared to go home with you," he said dully as he tapped on the door and walked into her room. Kara smiled and beckoned him in. He could hardly stand to see the edges of her hair singed, the soot still streaked across her forehead. It was only by the grace of God she hadn't been seriously burned, or worse.

"The dogs are okay," she said. "Chase told me."

"They're tough, for sure."

"I was telling Franco about the tarp and the yellow thread. I don't think he believed me. My phone photo wasn't very sharp, but I told him the answer has to be in those caves."

"I think you're right."

"You do?" She straightened, but it started a coughing fit. He quickly poured her a glass of water.

"No more laughing," he said with mock sternness.

"Check. It was just that you looked so reluctant to tell me you thought I was right."

Beau returned her glass to the table and took her hands in his. After a deep breath, he started in. "Kara, I'm going to the caves again."

Her eyes, shimmering hazel pools, lit up. "The answer has to be there. I'll—"

He spoke over her. "By myself."

She shook her head. "I want to help."

"I know. And I'm grateful, so grateful to have a…friend like you, but it's too much. There have been too many close calls. You could have died in that shed. Pioneer Day is over and you need to go home."

"I figured you'd say that, but my brothers can

help with security now. And the sheriff will assign an officer. They'll—"

"Kara…" His sharp tone made her flinch. He swallowed. "I don't want you here anymore." It hurt to say it, as if he were spitting out a burning coal.

She reached out to him. "You're scared. I am too, but we're close, and you don't have to face this alone."

He squeezed her fingers and kissed the tips of them, the faint scent of smoke that clung to her skin tickled his nose. "You have to go home with your family."

"But you can't manage it all on your own, the hatchery, the threats…"

"I can and I will, and that's how it has to be. I'll call you…after everything is resolved." If it ever was…

Her flicker of pain lashed at him. "You're shutting me out again."

"For your protection this time. Please, just accept it."

There was a question in her expression. What was the real motivation for his sending her away? A deep-down answer echoed in his own heart about how he felt, what he wanted, where life would take him if he asked her to be by his side, but she'd already been made promises to his best friend, the forever kind that Kyle hadn't been able to deliver. And with Beau's addled brain, he doubted he could either. He opened his mouth and the words tumbled out. "Kyle wouldn't have understood if I let anything happen to you."

Her face fell and he recognized his own cowardice. Putting Kyle between them. Not saying what he should have…

*I would never forgive myself.*

*I have to know you're safe.*

*Because of how I feel about you…*

He leaned closer but it was too late. The damage was done. She'd let go of his hand, turned her head away from him. "All right. If that's what you want," she murmured.

*It isn't…*

But it was the only way to make sure Kara Wolfe wasn't hurt anymore.

His heart ripped in two as he left her room.

Chase looked up as he trudged past, reading his expression, and he nodded once to show that Beau had made the right decision.

No, it hadn't been right, what he'd done. He'd wounded Kara deeply and his soul ached.

But he could think of no other way.

Because he was going to find out what was hidden in those caves and what had happened to him and his mother.

And it was clear someone was willing to risk everything to try and stop him.

That someone had to be close to home, a familiar face to anyone else.

But would he even recognize the danger when it came?

Before it was too late?

# FOURTEEN

Kara's lungs burned and her eyes watered as Chase drove her back to the hatchery to collect her gear and vehicle.

"We don't have to do it now. Garrett and I can get your car for you later. Let me take you home so Mom can fuss over you."

It was the last thing she wanted. All her hopes had evaporated. She'd not helped unravel the mystery of whatever happened to Ree or Beau all those years ago. Pioneer Day had ended in shambles, and she was not even sure of the status of the property Ree had entrusted her to sell. But deeper down, she was devastated about an entirely different matter. Beau didn't want to be with her because the shadow of his best friend Kyle would forever remain between them.

Because Beau would keep it there.

Tears pricked her eyelids as they drove onto the property, where Garrett stood waiting with Millie and Phil. The odor of charred wood still hung in the air. A light shone from Sonia and John's place, but no one came out. Vince's cabin was dark. She shuddered, considering what had almost happened in his shed. As far as she knew, the police hadn't yet tracked him down.

She hurried to the eager dogs, bending and fawning, hiding her face in their fur, which Phil endured for a few moments. "I'm so glad you're not hurt, babies. I love you."

Her brothers must have understood she didn't want to talk because they quietly loaded up their things and the drones and carried her suitcase to the van. When it was stowed, Garrett walked to her car with the keys in hand while Chase slid behind the wheel of the Security Hounds vehicle.

"How about I drive you, Sis?" Garrett said with a wink. "Chauffeur service. Much better than Chase. He's an absolute menace."

She shook her head. "Thank you, but I want to be alone, okay?"

Garrett hesitated, shooting a look at his brother.

"I'll be right behind you," she said quickly.

Her tone must have been convincing because they climbed into the van and headed down the road. She trailed in her car, the dogs lying together in the back seat. Her mind wandered over the deadly fire. If only the tarp and its missing piece hadn't been destroyed. Would it have provided proof of a crime? Indicated that Vince had been dumping something in the caves and concealed the tarp with the yellow thread in his shed afterward? Had he struck Beau down that night?

But Vince loved Ree. Why would he hurt her son? How would Vince explain what Millie had scented near his home?

It all remained a depressing unknown. They drove slowly off the hatchery property and she tried not to acknowledge that it would likely be a very long time before she returned, if ever.

She cracked the window to enjoy the splash of the tiny, wriggling fish once more. The miles grew steeper, winding around the mountain as she followed the Security Hounds van.

Sonia. John. Vince. Natalie. Was one of them responsible? If so, then Beau could literally have a potential murderer on his grounds.

The van vanished around the corner as she stopped to allow a possum to waddle across the road, and her thoughts drifted back across the few days she'd spent at the hatchery. Something nagged at her.

What?

The tarp in Vince's shed made no sense. With police around and the Security Hounds team on the premises, why would Vince keep an incriminating piece of evidence in his own backyard?

*His own backyard...*

Her mouth fell open as she recalled Sonia's comment about Ree.

*And she indulged me because I complained that we were crammed into the one-bedroom unit when a single guy was in the two-bedroom, and she convinced Vince to switch.*

Sonia and John had lived in that unit until just before Beau's attack.

Kara yanked the car over and thumbed in a text to her brothers: I think it's either Sonia or John, or maybe both of them. Beau needs to be warned.

The tiny exclamation point told her there was no service.

She tried dialing, but her call would not go through. Should she speed to catch up with the van? Turn around?

Heart pounding, she checked her watch. Would Beau be back at the hatchery? Heading for the caves? With fingers gone icy, she dialed his phone with no better result.

Beau wouldn't know what he was walking into.

Her stomach balled up tight. And when he saw his mother's employees approaching, he wouldn't even recognize them as enemy or friend.

Risk or no risk, the wrath of her brothers aside, she had to arm Beau with the truth. She pressed

Send on the text to her brothers again, and once more got no signal.

The dogs shifted in the back as she spun the car into a U-turn. Chase would realize soon enough that she wasn't following and he'd come to see why. All she had to do was find Beau and stop him from going to the caves alone.

She sped along the mountain road, expecting to see her brothers in the rearview mirror, but she careened onto the hatchery property solo. Her heart lurched when she saw Big Blue in the driveway. The office door was locked and Beau did not answer when she pounded on it. She tried to phone once more, but it went to voicemail. The two employee residences were quiet and dark.

There was only one place she would find him.

Quickly she messaged her brothers and told them her plans, praying the text would be delivered. Millie was eager to set off along the trail to the caves, as was Phil. It wasn't completely dark yet, but the shadows loomed large. She peered through her binoculars, and her heart leapt in her throat. Beau was making his way across the overlook in preparation to head down into the valley and explore the caves. She could hurry, get within shouting distance.

She and the dogs moved along the trail, alternately running and slowing to catch their breath. Twice she stopped and located him in her binoculars, but she was still too far away to catch his attention with a shout. She'd almost caught up when he reached the top of the overlook, but he outpaced her, and carrying Millie cost her time.

She lost sight of him again as he dropped down into the valley, where he'd parallel the river and reach the Mesquite Trail. He didn't hear her shouts either.

A little farther, maybe a half mile more, that's all she needed. Hopefully he would stop and give her a chance to close the distance. The dogs galloped on next to her, and when they made it to the shallower section and splashed across the river, Phil managed it with only a little reluctance. Soon they were passing the place where Ree was struck down and they'd been subjected to gunfire. She saw Beau, for one quick second, then they were scrambling to catch him again. By the time she closed the gap, she was completely out of breath, too winded to shout out as he descended into the caves with a rope ladder anchored to a tall prong of jutting granite near the opening. Where had the ladder come from? She'd not seen him carrying it.

A flood of fear urged her on and she yelled and sprinted to the opening of the cave just as Beau disappeared into the dark maw.

"Beau!" she called down. "Stop right this minute."

"Kara?"

She leaned over, hearing him calling out another question.

Two big hands shoved her from behind. The dogs barked furiously as she dropped into the cavern.

The swirl of dark hair confirmed it was Kara just before she crashed into him, and they both fell with a splash into several feet of frigid water. He righted himself, spluttering, and grabbed for her. She emerged, gasping against the cold and spitting out water.

"Someone pushed me in."

They looked up to see the ladder flung loose, plummeting down, a flash of a male face. Whose? He pulled her aside a moment before the ladder landed with a splash. The barking carried from up above.

"Away," Kara sternly commanded the dogs. She was trying to keep them from being pushed in or killed by whoever had tossed her in, likely Vince, the AWOL employee with the tarp in his shed.

Beau shouted, rage overtaking his frozen limbs. "Vince, if that's you, be a man and show yourself!"

"They switched," Kara said with a cough. "It's John. Maybe Sonia too."

"What?"

"John Partridge. Sonia and John switched cabins. They were living in Vince's place when you were attacked. One of them must have left the tarp there."

"John!" Beau roared.

No answer, only the murmur of the freezing water swirling around their knees. The reality of the situation was dire. The snowmelt was unbearably cold. Desperately he splashed around in search of a place where they could climb out or he could at least get her above the waterline. His boot struck something, and he played the light down in the swirling liquid. Kara followed his gaze.

A gleam of yellow shone like a broken blossom. He bent closer, and a ruined face peered up at him, the features bloated and partially decomposed.

Kara reeled back, her hand pressed to her mouth. "Oh no."

"Who is it?" he said. "I can't recognize him."

"I think it's… Rocklin Clark, Natalie's ex-husband."

Beau whistled. "So it's Natalie? Has she been lying about him leaving her, living in Europe?"

"Obviously John was impersonating Rocklin, because I heard the broker supposedly talking to him on the phone." Her lips were trembling.

Beau was thinking through the implications. If John killed Rocklin and dumped the body, then his mom witnessed something amiss…

From above, there was a scuffling sound, a male voice speaking angrily. "I've had enough."

"So have I," a woman's voice replied. He knew that throaty alto. Natalie Clark.

John's voice again. "We can't…"

The whap of something metal on flesh, a sickening thud… Instinctively, Beau grabbed Kara as John's body crashed into the rock wall before it hurtled toward them and landed with a sickening thump and splash inches from where they huddled.

He pulled a flashlight from his pocket and shined it on the fallen man.

"Oh no," Kara whispered.

John Partridge stared back at him, eyes open in death, blood pouring from the place where his skull had been caved in. Beau checked for a pulse to be certain. Nothing.

"Why?" Kara breathed, sounding as if she was fighting not to gag. "He was her accomplice."

Beau strung the details together. "Mom was going to sell. Develop the trail. That would mean Rocklin's body might be discovered. Natalie offered to buy that portion of property to prevent that happening, but Mom declined. Natalie and John probably intended to move him, but the snowmelt flooded the caves and they had to wait."

The horror washed over him until he shut it down. Every moment they remained where they were, they inched closer to death. "I think there's a back way out of here and we need to find it. Can you walk?"

Her nod was faint. He swept her close, her trembling like a river running through both of them. His heart squeezed. "You should be safe at home. Why did you come back, Henny Penny?"

"I couldn't let you face it alone."

He didn't hesitate then. He kissed her deeply before he squeezed her to his chest, praying that her act of bravery would not come at the expense of her life.

Their legs were swallowed in the freezing water. Hypothermia would not be long in overtaking them. *Focus on escape.* But he saw nothing except black rock all around. There was not a single detail about the crypt-like space that felt at all familiar.

Kara cocked her head. "Did you hear that?" A faint bark echoed along the passage. "It's Millie."

"Millie!" they both yelled at once.

The answer was a louder mingling of both canine voices. Millie and Phil, like two homing beacons. They'd found another entrance, which, he prayed, would prove to be an exit.

Beau led Kara around a prong of granite until they entered a narrower passageway.

Kara encouraged the dogs to bark periodically to help them along. "Beau, if John was her accomplice, why kill him?"

"Loose ends," he said grimly. "Like we are. With all of us dead, there's no one to suspect her."

The tunnel led them to an opening the size of a manhole cover. Millie and Phil were crowded together, outlined against the darkening sky, whining at them to hurry up already.

Natalie might be out there waiting for her prey to emerge. "I need to go first, in case."

With great difficulty, he squeezed along the slippery rock, and with painful scrapes to the shoulders, jammed his way clear. The dogs immediately swarmed him as he rolled onto all fours and sprang to his feet, reaching for his handgun.

But there was no sign of Natalie or anyone else.

He dropped to his stomach, extending his arms until Kara could grab hold. Inch by inch, he pulled her free. Millie and Phil yowled and licked her face until she calmed them.

Phone quivering in his frozen hands, Beau tried to dial 911. "No signal here. Come on." He helped her up. "Can you make it back?"

She nodded. "Watch me."

He chuckled, and they began to move as quickly as they could, their wet clothes weighing them down. It was an agonizing hike, and Beau could barely manage to carry Millie up and over the rocky outlook stairs, but at long last, they approached the office.

A woman's voice floated out the open front door, and he jerked a look at Kara.

"That's Natalie Clark and she's talking to my brothers." They crept closer, the dogs in silent mode.

"I've been trying to find John," Natalie said. "He's been acting so weird. I think maybe he might have set that fire in the shed." She paused. "I know this sounds crazy, but I'm beginning to wonder if he did something to my husband. That he's been pretending to be Rocklin and make me think he's in Europe all this time. Faking texts and calls."

"Where's my sister?" a strong voice demanded.

*Chase*, Kara mouthed to him.

"I saw her taking the dogs up the road toward the fire lookout," Natalie lied.

Beau moved Kara behind him and burst through the door. Natalie screamed and shoved a kitchen chair at Beau. He stumbled over it, knocking into Chase. Natalie used the opportunity to hurtle toward Kara.

Before Beau could spring to his feet again, Phil cannonballed into Natalie's legs, and she flipped over his body and onto her stomach. Kara immediately dropped to her knees, pinning Natalie with her full weight until Beau, Chase and Garrett made it to her side to restrain the woman.

Kara climbed free, calming the dogs as the amber lights announced the arrival of the police.

Natalie glared at Beau.

He knew the face he was looking at—this woman who'd pretended to be his mother's friend—was the face of a killer. But someone else claimed his attention, a gentle, stricken face of the person who'd refused to give up on him.

Kara cried as he folded her close.

"It's over," he said. At long last, the evil that had been hidden right under their noses had been unmasked.

Closing his eyes, he kissed the top of her head and let her cry onto his chest.

Kara arrived at the hatchery with the dogs on a brilliant Friday morning. Before she got out, she sent Beau a selfie and captioned it with her name. Looking for my friend Beau, she texted, half teasing and ensuring he'd know who she was. She reminded herself too. *You're his friend, Kara Wolfe.* It still hurt that he'd decided that was where their relationship would remain, but she was grateful to have him back in her life. She'd had the love of one incredible man, and that would be her solace. A woman could do a lot worse, but the pain persisted, humming just under her ribs.

Beau met her by her car and greeted the dogs. Millie slobbered on him enthusiastically before her nose led her away to sniff the raceway where the fish wriggled. Phil kept pace, Millie's silent shadow, watchful as always.

Kara saw Beau examining her hands, as he often did, and the smile that came over his face as his brain made the recognition. She reached out and squeezed his fingers.

"I'm so glad to hear about your mom."

"Me too." His eyes were a brighter shade of blue now, the color teased to its fullest by relief. "She's itching to come home. Docs said tomorrow maybe. She'll be weak for a long time, but Vince and I are here to help with whatever she needs."

Kara's gaze drifted to Vince's cabin, then the Partridges' unit, now unoccupied. Sonia had gone to stay with her sister while arrangements were made for John's funeral. Franco had ascertained that though Sonia suspected a relationship between Natalie and John, she'd been unaware he'd murdered Rocklin on Natalie's behalf. She'd also been clueless that he'd snuck away from their camping vacation to cause the landslide that almost killed Beau and Kara. Likely, John and Natalie had worked together to take Ree out of the picture when she'd seen one or both of them near the caves trying to move Rocklin's body before the improvements began. The two conspirators had fallen out, or John had threatened to come clean perhaps, which explained why she'd bludgeoned John and thrown him into the caves. She hadn't confessed to anything, but it was clear that she'd been helping herself to Rocklin's money while pretending to receive communications from him. Even the call the police had made to the hotel room had been John using the phone he'd taken from Rocklin's body as part of the ruse.

The other clues fell into place.

John had a paintball gun. Likely he'd also tampered with the log bridge, caused the flood on the property, and locked Kara in the shed and set it on fire, knowing his DNA was probably on the tarp he'd returned after hauling Rocklin to the caves.

Natalie had tried to poison the dogs and swung at Kara with the shovel. She'd probably taken the rifle shots at them or had John do it.

Two murderers who'd gotten in deeper with every lie they'd told.

Kara shook away the horrifying thoughts.

Ree would be back home soon. She'd recovered enough to explain she'd intended to sell the property and accept a marriage proposal from Vince after Beau insisted on staying away. She'd thought it would be the only thing she could do for Beau, to give him part of the proceeds to restart his life and try and do the same with hers, sans hatchery.

Beau held on as his mother cried through her confession. He'd kissed her and declined. "Mom, I'm not taking a penny. The hatchery is yours and so are the proceeds."

Kara sighed as she remembered the tender emotion between mother and son. She settled on the low cement wall and Beau sat next to her. Millie shoved her floppy jowls over the side of the raceway to track the fish. Kara felt Beau watching as she tipped her face to the sun, catching the tension in the lines of his jaw.

"What's up, buttercup?" she teased.

He shrugged. "Trying to memorize your beautiful face, like always."

*Beautiful.* She ducked her chin. "You don't need to. I'll send you a zillion selfies of me with my saggy dogs."

Her tone was light, but he didn't smile. Instead he got up and turned away from her, chin dropping, arms folded across his broad chest.

"I'm not the same man I used to be."

Such heartbreak in his tone, such resignation.

She rose, wishing he would meet her eyes. "That's true, Beau. You're not."

She heard his gusty sigh. "No one stays the same down here on planet Earth."

He shook his head. "I'm damaged. I can't recognize people."

"Not with your eyes."

He paused. "I have this recurring nightmare that I'm walking down the aisle to the woman I'm going to marry. I lift her veil and I don't recognize her."

She turned him in her direction, then took his hand and brushed it over her hair, her cheek. "These things you can touch now will change. Skin wrinkles, hair turns gray, eyes dim, hands get arthritic and age-spotted. None of it will stay this way."

He looked at their joined hands as she went on.

"Someday I won't look anything like I do right now, and my children or grandchildren will see pictures of me and say, 'That's *you*, Granny?'"

He shot a quizzical glance at her now.

"You know that old song?" She hummed a few bars. "They will know we are Christians by our love? That's what I pray. That people will know me for how I love." She paused. "Will you know me that way, Beau? For the moments we spent together as kids, for the connection we made as we searched for your mother?"

She heard his breath hitch.

"Yes." His eyes were a shimmer of azure. "Since I came back, I let thoughts of Kyle stand between us, but it was fear, Kara. Fear of what I can't do anymore."

"Close your eyes, Beau."

His brow quirked with a question.

"Just close them."

He did. His expression was torn between hope and fear, and something deeper that made her pulse hitch and her breath grow shallow. Upward from her heart surged a cascade of memories. She gripped his fingers and squeezed. "Listen to my voice. Do you know me, Beau?"

He pressed his cheek to her hands, breathing hard, silent.

"Do you know me?" she repeated.

"I know you." His voice broke. "I'll always know you with my soul."

And then he opened his eyes.

At the precise same instant, they both said, "I love you."

The words were like a shout of hope.

His smile was radiant, relieved, joyful, all the emotions that rolled through her. She laughed. Maybe that was how God really meant for people to know one another, by who they were, their acts of love, expressions of his goodness that had nothing to do with appearances.

He scooped her into a tight hug. She was unable to speak a word, breathing him in as he held her close, basking in the knowledge that he loved her.

"Kara, I'm going to stay here and run the hatchery for mom."

She snuggled closer and spoke against his neck. "I'm thrilled. If you need the help of a real estate agent and a couple of raggedy hounds, just whistle."

He pulled her away and bent to kiss her. "I do need you. Every day," he said. "I'm going to rebuild my life here, one hour at a time. And I'm praying that you'll be with me in it, if I haven't messed things up too much."

She held up a thumb and forefinger. "Just a little, Beau O'Connor, but nothing we can't fix up, shipshape."

He kissed her again, and she felt all the love and tenderness racing inside her like the little fish wriggling through the clear mountain waters.

\* \* \* \* \*

*If you enjoyed this story by Dana Mentink,
be sure to pick up the previous books in
the Security Hounds miniseries*

Tracking the Truth
Fugitive Search
Hunted on the Trail

*Available now from Love Inspired Suspense!*

Dear Reader,

How fascinating it is that we invest so much value in the human face. We take it for granted that our brains will immediately recognize someone by the merest glimpse. It was interesting to write about a character who isn't able to do that. It made me consider how our faces morph and change, like the rest of our bodies, but that doesn't matter to God. He knows us, truly and deeply, both our sinful and saintly tendencies, and He loves us. Isn't that an incredible comfort, to be fully known and fully loved?

I hope you have enjoyed Beau and Kara's adventures. The next book in the series will feature impetuous brother Chase and his big lug of a dog, Tank. Come along on the escapade with me and we'll see what God has in store!

God bless!
*Dana Mentink*